GIANT BANANA OVER TEXAS

DARKLY HUMOROUS TALES BY MARK NUTTER

Cover art by Michael Johnson

Author photo by Craig Semetko

"The Man of a Trillion Faces" first appeared in *Havok Magazine.*

"My Year with the Perfect Family" first appeared in *Mystery Weekly Magazine.*

Print ISBN: 978-1-66782-666-0
eBook ISBN: 978-1-66782-667-7

For Charlotte

CONTENTS

INTRODUCTION:
WHY A GIANT BANANA?

In 2008, the Argentinian artist César Sáez proposed the creation and launch of a banana-shaped, 300-meter-long airship that would hover over the state of Texas. Even though he received $140,000 in grant money, Sáez never built his banana. Seems it was a hoax. Nevertheless, I love the concept, a grand and silly gesture, a glorious celebration of pointlessness. I aspire to do something similar with this collection—and that's the closest thing to a statement of artistic intent you'll ever get from me.

BEWARE THE GRATEFUL MAN

Look.

Here comes the Grateful Man.

He's smiling.

He says, "I am grateful for the sunny sky."

See how dark billows gather and pour torrents of rain on the Grateful Man.

He continues to smile. He says, "I am grateful for liquid sunshine that makes the flowers bloom."

See how the deluge sweeps away topsoil, taking with it tulips, daffodils, marigolds, and calla lilies.

"The rain carries the flowers down the hill so that people at the bottom can enjoy them, and for this I am grateful."

The flowers swirl and disappear down a sewer grate.

"I am grateful for sewers," says the Grateful Man.

He is relentless.

Beware the Grateful Man.

* * *

My name is Lance Tinley. After ten years in New York, racing around Manhattan with the other rats, my wife Barb and I were burnt out.

"Lance," she said, "I hope you're not going to say, 'It's time for us to make a fresh start.'"

"Why don't you want me to say it?"

3

"Because *I* want to say it!"

She said it. Then she squealed and I squealed, and we jumped up and down for an hour.

We sold our condo in Chelsea and looked for the ideal upstate town to begin our new lives.

Slag City was a Rust Belt town, no longer thriving, which meant there were real estate bargains galore. We bought a three-story building on Main Street. Our plan was to live on the upper floors and use the first floor for our new business: Creative Names by Lance and Barb, Inc.

I loved drinking craft beers with names like Hop Devil, and Hop Demon, and Double Dark Hop Demon. I thought, I could do that, I could name beers. I would become a professional craft beer namer. Slag City alone had six craft breweries.

Barb always loved the funny names of hair salons like Julius Scissors and Shearlock Combs, so she would handle that end of our naming business.

We were so excited about starting our own business that we failed to notice the town's homeless problem, as well as its domestic abuse and murder and obesity and alcohol problems.

One day a fat man in an ill-fitting suit came into our shop. I'd seen him in the town square, conning the homeless with three-card monte.

He was trembling.

"I need a drink bad," he said, looking at the sample labels on the wall. "Gimme a pint of Hop, Skip, and a Jump."

"Sorry," I said, "I don't sell beer, I just sell beer names."

"That's fine, I'm trying to cut down anyway. Gimme the label."

I served him, then asked, "Are you okay?"

"Do I look okay?" he said, nervously licking the sticky side. "I heard a rumor. *He's* coming back. Same again."

I served him his second label and said, "Who is *he*?"

He stared at me. "You really don't know, do you?"

The fat man pointed out the front window with a shaking hand.

"Who do you think made Slag City the way it is?"

"Someone named Slag?"

The fat man snorted. He backed up to the door.

"You'll see. He'll come back, and then you'll see."

And with that he was gone, off to find another beer-label shop.

"That was weird," I said.

"How's this for a hair salon name?" said Barb. "The Hoppy Hairport."

"I don't think you should use the word 'hop' in a hair salon name. That's just for craft beers."

"Okay. Thanks for the feedback."

I considered the domestic abuse and drug deals and the other Slag City problems, many of which were visible through our front window.

"This town really is sort of depressed. And the fat guy said one man was responsible. Who was he talking about?"

"Beats me. You know," said Barb, taking down the hair salon signs with the word "hop" in them, "usually in these towns there's an irascible old man who can tell you the town's history. I saw that in a movie."

"*Jaws*?"

"Yes, and *Star Wars* too."

"I bet we can find an irascible old man at the local tavern."

"Yes!" said Barb, getting excited. "He'll be sitting in the corner, scratching his stubbly beard."

"And spitting on the floor."

"What are we waiting for?!"

* * *

We hung a sign on our front door that read, GONE FISHIN'—FOR INFORMATION.

In the town square, the fat guy was running the same three-card monte on the same homeless people who apparently had yet to learn their lesson.

At the end of Main Street stood the Slag City Tavern.

As we entered the old dark establishment, we were assaulted by the odors of peanuts, stale vomit, fresh vomit, and craft beer.

Our eyes adjusted to the dark, and we saw him. The irascible old guy. Then our eyes further adjusted, and we saw more irascible old guys. There were more irascible old guys in the bar than there were corners for them to sit in.

"Pick one," I said to Barb. She pointed to an old guy with more teeth than the others.

"My name is Old Peck," he rasped, "and I'll tell you the town's history if you buy me a shot of rotgut hooch."

"You sure you wouldn't rather have a pint of"—I squinted at the craft beer menu behind the bar—"Hop-a-Doodle-Doo?"

Old Peck vomited on the floor.

"Rotgut hooch," I said to the bartender.

We took our seats. Old Peck began his tale.

"This used to be a thriving Rust Belt town," he began. "Everybody worked at the plant. We made not only rust-colored belts but sienna, tawny, burnt umber—every shade of brown you can imagine."

He took a sip of his hooch, coughed, and continued.

"Everybody was happy. America was on top. We wore bell-bottoms and danced to REO Speedwagon. Everyone owned a pocket calculator. We didn't think life could get any better."

Old Peck's face clouded.

"Then everything changed."

He looked at me with pleading eyes. "Gimme a pint of Hoppy Hoppy Joy Joy."

Old Peck sniffed his beer, vomited, and continued.

"One day we decided to have a little fair in the town square. The theme of the fair was 'It's an REO Speedwagon World.' There would be hot dogs, cotton candy, games with prizes, and lots of dancing to REO Speedwagon.

"There was this new guy in town. We called him Smiley 'cause he smiled all the time. He worked on the belt-buckle line, and he was terrible, always putting buckles on crooked or backward, but I guess he got the job 'cause of his smile.

"Well, he was setting up cutouts of the band with the faces removed so people could put their heads in the holes and pretend they were in REO Speedwagon. And he suddenly stopped.

"'Hey, everybody!' he shouted out to us, smiling his big smiley smile. 'I just want to say I'm grateful, so grateful, for everything. Grateful for this wonderful town. Grateful for the belt factory. Grateful for our prosperity and our families. I'm grateful for this beautiful sunshiny day. Grateful for my bell-bottoms and my pocket calculator. Man, am I ever grateful!'

The old man fell silent.

"So what happened?" I said.

Old Peck took a sip of Hoppy Hoppy Joy Joy and managed to keep it down.

"The sky turned dark. Rain poured down. A wind blew away our pocket calculators. Then it blew away our houses and our wives and our children."

"Must've been a strong wind," said Barb.

"You ain't lyin', sister. All of a sudden, we went from having everything to having nothing. We couldn't believe it. And then he did it again."

"Who did what again?" I said.

"Smiley," said Old Peck bitterly. "He said, 'Sure, the wind blew away everything we have. But look at us.'"

Old Peck was shaking so much his teeth rattled.

"Then he said, 'At least we have our'"—Old Peck swallowed hard—"'health.'"

"I was there," said a one-armed old guy who had been listening in.

"I knew it was trouble when he said it," said another old guy with no legs.

"Brap ssss ttt," said a fourth old guy through a faulty mechanical voice box.

Barb and I glanced around at the bar filled with the aging, unhealthy, unsightly victims of Smiley's gratitude.

"We did our best to run him out of town," said Old Peck. "Not an easy task with our lungs failing and our limbs dropping off. But we did it!"

"Yeah!" said the other old guys.

"And he's never coming back!" declared Old Peck.

"That's not what the big guy in the town square said," I told them.

"You mean Three-Card Monte Monty? He's called Three-Card Monty for short. What did Monty say?"

"There's a rumor *he* was coming back," I said.

Panic gripped the room. The bar patrons ordered drinks and knocked them back faster than the bartender could serve them.

"Everybody be on guard," warned Old Peck. "If he shows up again, he'll find something else to be grateful for, and we're doomed."

"What does he look like?" I asked. "Big smile?"

"You've seen him!" shouted Old Peck.

Everyone ran back to the bar for another drink.

"I'm just guessing," I said.

"Brrr zpp," said Faulty Voice Box.

* * *

Barb and I walked back to our shop, past the town square, where Monty was returning money to the homeless so he could con them again.

"I thought being grateful brought more good things into your life," said Barb.

"Me too! I thought gratitude was a good investment. I wrote that down in my gratitude journal."

I was glad we didn't stay at the Slag City Tavern, drinking with Old Peck and the limbless patrons, because work was piling up. When we checked our voice mail, we had dozens of requests for names, requests that kept us busy for a month. The best one I came up with was Hoppy Days Are Beer Again. Barb hit a home run with Bangs! Bangs! Your Dreads!

As busy as we were, we never let down our guard. We kept an eye out for anyone who smiled, or anyone named Smiley, or anyone named Grinny, in case he was using an alias.

Thanks to my clever names, the six breweries in Slag City were thriving. Now everyone in Slag City had jobs making craft beer: Old Peck, the old guys at the tavern, even the homeless who were still homeless, because even with steady paychecks, they kept losing money to Monty.

With this newfound wealth, there was a demand for more hair salons, because wealthy people got their hair done several times a day. People came from all over to open salons, and Barb could barely keep up with the demand. Names like Hair Pie and Hair Up Your Ass were not her best work, but no one cared.

The next logical step was to make Slag City the new state capital. Thousands of workers came to build the sleek new modern capital building. Of course, with all the new workers in town, that meant more craft beer breweries and hair salons, plus more casinos and whorehouses.

The revitalization of Slag City was national news, and it wasn't long before Hollywood came calling, thinking our story would make a great movie. They filmed all the interiors right here in town. The Slag City exteriors were done on a Hollywood soundstage. They asked us what movie stars should play us on the big screen. I was realistic, never expecting to be played by Brad Pitt. Instead, my character was a digitized version of a camel with the head of thirties character actor Edward Everett Horton, which is easy to do these days.

Everybody in town got to go to the Academy Awards. It was a thrill to sit in the audience and hear them say, "The Oscar for Best Picture goes to . . . *Slag City: A New Hop.*" (I got to name the film.)

Everyone from Slag City came onstage and gave a little acceptance speech. The orchestra didn't dare play us off, not with all the limbless old guys up there.

When it was my turn to speak—I don't know, maybe it was the bright lights, or the glamorous movie star company, or Barb standing next to me wearing a gown that made her look like a soft-serve ice cream cone—I began:

"I'd like to thank the academy . . ."

And then time stopped. I saw everything clearly. The success we were enjoying was not an accident. It had a single cause:

My gratitude journal.

It's true. If you want more good things in your life, you must express gratitude in your journal for what you already have. So that's what I did.

I felt a smile growing on my face. I couldn't stop it. I couldn't help myself.

"I am just so damn *grateful!*"

Then the earthquake hit.

* * *

Magnitude 7.5. Madness.

Even so, with people screaming and EMS workers combing through the wreckage of the Dolby Theatre, I still couldn't shut up.

"I'm grateful for these brave first responders . . ."

Who were unprepared for the aftershock that buried them under what remained of the Dolby Theatre roof.

"But mostly," I said, dusting myself off, my smile bigger than ever, "I am grateful for my wife, Barb . . ."

* * *

Look.

Here I come.

I say, "I am grateful for the clear blue sky."

See how the torrential rain washes away the topsoil and the flowers.

I say, "I am grateful for the second and third and fourth responders who I'm sure will find Barb once they save the movie stars."

Do I keep smiling? Of course I do. You can call me Smiley.

I'm coming to your town.

See you soon.

OBITUARY 101

Did my life have value and meaning? The professor said everyone's life did, but he barely knew me.

I raised my hand.

"Professor Landon?"

"Lucy, I'm not a professor, I'm just a teacher."

"I'm sorry."

"This isn't a university, it's a YMCA."

"I'm sorry."

"Please stop apologizing. Call me professor if you like."

"No, that would be wrong."

"Okay, call me Mr. Landon. What was your question?"

"I forgot."

I sunk back into my chair as Mr. Landon—who certainly looked like a professor—continued. He was saying, while some might consider writing their own obituary a morbid activity, it is in fact an opportunity to reaffirm our value as we enter Life's Third Act.

The eight silver-haired seniors in the class smiled Third Act smiles. I'm only thirty-two but maybe I was also entering my Third Act, following shorter, sadder First and Second Acts.

"Professor Landon? What if we don't want to reaffirm our value?"

"Why not?"

"I might have too much value, and reaffirming it could take all day." I don't think he bought it.

Professor Landon rubbed his beard.

"Why are you taking this class?"

"To write my obituary so my mother doesn't have to."

"You take care of your mother?"

"I haven't seen her in fourteen years. I just thought it would be nice to include my obituary in a Christmas card."

He nodded approvingly. "This could be a way for you to reconcile."

"I don't want to reconcile, I just want to send her a nice card."

Professor Landon cleaned his glasses with the edge of his vest.

"Lucy—and everyone else—we're going to use our obituaries to honor the highlights of our lives. That's your assignment for next week. Come back with a list of ten highlights."

"I'm awfully busy," I said.

He cleaned his glasses harder, staring at me.

"Five highlights."

"There was nothing in the class description about homework."

"See you next week," he snarled.

* * *

Life highlights. I'd try.

On my breaks from my job as a teller at the First Premier New Horizon Bank I sat in the employee lounge with pen and paper, ready to record highlights. I did that Tuesday and Wednesday. On Thursday I still had an empty pad. Trying to think of highlights was not a highlight.

Then on Friday I had a great idea. What if I listed the times I hurt less than others? Maybe those were highlights. The prospect excited me.

* * *

At Monday's class I waved my hand furiously in the air like a third grader who knew the answer and needed the bathroom, both.

"Lucy?"

I jumped to my feet.

"When I was seven my pet goldfish, Charlie, jumped out of his bowl, landed on the floor, and turned brown and crispy in the afternoon sun."

The only sound I heard was the air-conditioning.

"How is that a highlight?" said the professor.

"I thought I'd feel terrible—and I did—but not nearly as terrible as when my father accidentally stepped on my kitten Barney's head. So Charlie was a highlight, relatively speaking."

My enthusiasm was slipping away like dirty water down a bathtub drain.

"Let's see." I checked my notes with a trembling hand. "When I was eleven, I broke both kneecaps in gym class. . . ."

The class reflexively grabbed their knees or their knee replacements.

"And I realize that didn't hurt nearly as much as when I had seven teeth pulled without novocaine."

Some tried grabbing their knees and their teeth simultaneously.

"And . . . oh! When I was twenty-six my fiancé stole my car and my life savings and disappeared."

The old people gazed at the ceiling, the floor, anywhere but at me.

"Actually, I couldn't think of anything worse than the fiancé, so . . ."

I sat down in slow motion.

"Sorry."

"Who's next?" said the professor.

An energetic woman with a youthful face stood up.

"My name is Emma. I'm seventy-five years old."

Everyone but me went, "Ooh."

Emma held notes but didn't need to look at them. Show-off.

"I graduated from med school when I was twenty-one. I joined Doctors Without Borders. That's where I met my husband, Leonard, who also worked for Doctors Without Borders. We had three children, all girls, who all became doctors and now work for Doctors Without Borders. . . ."

Tuning Emma out, I considered saying I joined Friendly Bank Tellers Without Borders, then decided against it. I've never been out of the country, plus I'm not friendly, plus there is no such organization.

Emma was finally finishing.

"And it is my deepest desire that everyone leave the world a better place when they die. As I hope I've done."

Everybody went "ooh" again.

"That was beautiful, Emma," said Professor Landon. "How do you feel?"

"Peaceful. I feel like I can now act with greater clarity about my life's purpose."

I could feel the sweat under my arms and breasts and bottom.

"You've led a good life. You don't need to do anything more."

"But I'd like to, while I still have precious moments left."

Shut up, Emma, I screamed inside my head.

"Next week," said Professor Landon, "we'll hear more highlights. Lucy, just come in with one that isn't pitiful."

"Right. I'm on it."

* * *

Couldn't think of a thing.

Maybe there had been something in high school.

In my senior yearbook someone had drawn a caricature of me as a horse. I wondered if that was a highlight, since I liked horses more than the other animals people drew me as.

Nothing I thought of could compete with Emma, the filthy old whore.

* * *

At the next class, Emma's chair was empty.

"Sadly," said Professor Landon, "Emma met with a tragic accident."

Everyone went "Ooh," not much different from the "oohs" she got when she was alive.

"A doctor can still have an accident with a scalpel if they've had too much to drink or been accidentally heavily drugged."

We nodded. That was so true.

"At least she had a nice obituary," someone said.

"It *was* nice, wasn't it? So . . . " The professor rubbed his hands and licked his lips. "Let's hear some others."

A broad-shouldered guy named Stan reflected on how grateful he was to have coached Little League for forty-five years, seeing dozens of his kids go on to become professional ball players and federal judges.

A trim old woman named Mary revealed she spent six months on the space shuttle *Endeavor*, where she recorded a folk album and grew plants that would one day cure Alzheimer's.

An author named Warren had already turned his obituary into a novel, which was now on the *New York Times* best-seller list. He read us the rave reviews.

"Lucy?"

"Somebody drew me as horse."

"What?"

"I like horses," I whispered, as I shrank to the size of a paramecium.

* * *

Sitting in the employee lounge, I thought my horse highlight might've worked if I'd presented it with greater confidence. But probably not. The highlights other people in the class presented shared an important element—ministration to others.

Ministration. Of course! Why hadn't I thought of it before?

* * *

"I spent my life working with the poorest of the poor in Calcutta. I won the Nobel Peace Prize. Then I changed my name to Lucy."

"You're not Mother Teresa."

"Um. How can you be sure?"

"Mother Teresa is dead."

Suddenly tearful, I blubbered, "She had a really good obituary."

"You have to write your own, you can't steal someone else's."

Oh triple heck. Wiping my eyes, I had a look around. I had been so obsessed with my imaginary Nobel Prize I hadn't noticed every other seat but one was empty.

"Where are Stan and Mary and Warren?"

"They died."

He's joking, I thought. But Professor Landon had the same look on his face he had when he told me I wasn't Mother Teresa, so I knew it must be true.

"Their deaths were not unlike that of Doctors Without Borders Emma."

"Accidents with scalpels?"

"Similar. Mary had an accident with pruning shears she used on her Alzheimer's plants. Warren had a mishap with a fancy letter opener that looked like a scalpel. Stan was impaled with a baseball bat that had been sharpened to a point."

"Why would he sharpen a bat?"

"He was old, he could do what he wanted."

I felt bad for hating them because they had better life highlights. At least they had nice obituaries. Funny that as soon as they finished them . . .

Oh boy.

For the first time I noticed bloodstains on Professor Landon's vest, stains not there on the first day of class.

Pete, an easygoing man in his late seventies, began to rise.

I grabbed him by his sleeve and pulled him back.

"Don't."

"But I want to read my obituary."

"Lucy, let go of Pete."

Professor Landon pried my fingers off Pete's jacket. I collapsed back into my chair as he walked to the front of the room and began to read:

"I led a rich full life—"

Nice knowing you, Pete.

* * *

Doggone it. Had I known the course was run by a serial killer who couldn't murder his victims until they'd written their own obituaries—I could've saved three hundred dollars.

The responsible thing to do was to contact the police. And that's what I decided to do. Together the cops and I would put this sicko professor away for good.

* * *

"Welcome back, Lucy."

"Thanks, Professor."

The classroom was empty. Just me and him.

"I suppose Pete was killed in a scalpel accident."

"Far worse than driving and texting--is driving and holding a scalpel next to your jugular."

After making a mental note to never do that, I held up the pages of my finished work. My fear of reading in front of a crowd had disappeared—as had the crowd.

"I've led a pitiful life," I began. "I never realized just how pitiful before I enrolled in this course. But now I see it. And you know what? It took courage to look. I looked at myself honestly for the first time.

"Like Ringo's song that goes, 'What do you see when you turn out the light? I can't tell you but I know it's mine.'

"I accept myself more now than I ever have, even when I was Mother Teresa.

"Okay, I'm done."

Professor Landon smiled.

Mom, if you're reading this you should know that this is my obituary, and I'm dead.

My last act was to call the police and give them my address. I hope they arrest him before he gets to me, but I don't think they will, because I see his car out there in the driveway. Here he comes.

No wait, calling the police wasn't my last act, it was my second-to-last. My last was to review the Obituary Writing Course on Yelp. I liked gaining greater acceptance of my life. I didn't like knowing I would be killed. Two stars.

GOD EMBRACES POLYTHEISM

And lo, God didst create the world in six days, the earth and heavens, the stars and planets, the fishes of sea, the beasts of the fields, man and woman, anything you can think of, created he it.

And on the seventh day God rested, or intended to anyway, however never had he a free moment to kick back and grab a nap, because he needed to keep the rivers flowing and the tide going in and out and the grass growing and the flowers blooming and he was so overwhelmed he forgot to make the sun come up.

And hence the earth was plunged into darkness, until God dropped the other things he was doing and focused on the sun, and as a result the rivers stagnated and turned yellow and the grass came up stubbly and flower petals had holes in them and didn't look very nice, and many other things of the earth came out looking half-assed.

And when Adam and Eve thanked God for the bounty of the earth, he could tell their hearts weren't in it.

And lo, God was inspired, and he didst make of the clay of the earth a business consultant named Joan Kearney.

And Joan Kearney didst examine the shoddy work God had done recently, the trees with runty leaves and the stars that flickered on and off.

And Joan Kearney sayeth unto God, "Come into my office and sit ye down."

And she sayeth unto him, "Almighty Father, you're spreading yourself too thin. You must stop micromanaging and learn to delegate."

And God sayeth unto Joan Kearney, "I cannot delegate. There is no one I trust, for I am the only god."

And Joan Kearney sayeth, "Then you must make another god."

And she didst take God by the hand and lead him down to earth to a mountain stream, where bathed a young maiden, naked.

And Joan Kearney sayeth unto God, "You must transform yourself into a bull and copulate with her."

And God sayeth, "Why a bull?"

And Joan Kearney sayeth, "So as not to frighten her."

And lo, God didst assume the form of a bull and appeared unto the young maiden, whose name was Sharon.

And Sharon didst not fear the bull, because she was bent.

And God and Sharon didst copulate, and lo, Sharon bore God a male child, who she called Jeff.

And now there were two gods upon the earth—God and Jeff.

And Joan Kearney sayeth unto God, "Delegate unto Jeff a job."

And God considered giving unto Jeff the job of making the sun rise, but then decided he'd rather do the big stuff himself.

And God sayeth unto Jeff, "Thou shalt attach yellow lichens to tree trunks, and thou shalt be the god of that."

And Jeff went off to do the lichens, and God was able to kick back and take a load off.

And it was not long before God had to attend to a host of things, not the lichens because Jeff was on it, but all the other things, causing God to once again forget to make the sun come up.

And Joan Kearney sayeth, "Make another god."

And this time God took the shape of a stallion, and Sharon was also good with that.

And Sharon bore God a daughter who she called Connie.

And Connie was given the job of managing the slurping sounds waves make when they wash over sand.

And lo, God was getting the hang of delegating.

And God didst create more gods and goddesses with other maidens besides Sharon, because she drew the line at bulls and stallions.

And the land didst fill with temples to the many gods born of the seed of the original God:

Larry, god of mosquitoes in your ear.

Nancy, goddess of clouds that looked like animal faces.

Ben, god of tooth decay.

Jessica, goddess of gravel.

The twins Albert and Allison, god and goddess of the brown spots on bananas.

And many more.

And God found himself with nothing to do, because he wasn't interested in the big stuff anymore either and had given the sunrise to the new god Ernie.

And this was fine with God, who had made everything and everybody and thought he deserved a vacation, and so taketh he one.

And after many generations there arose in the desert a tribe of people called the Industrialites, who were the first entrepreneurs.

And the Industrialites were distraught, for they longed to be devout, but they were so busy designing, launching, and running new businesses they had not enough time to worship the ten thousand gods of the earth.

And the leader of the Industrialites, who was called Lyle J. French, sayeth unto his people, "We must summon the business consultant Joan Kearney."

And Joan Kearney didst appear to the Industrialites, and she was much impressed with the way the tribe set goals that were specific, measurable, achievable, realistic, and timely.

And Joan Kearney sayeth unto Lyle J. French, "What troubles thou?"

And Lyle J. French told her the Industrialites were unable to worship every single god, given the tribe's eighty-hour workweek.

And Joan Kearney sayeth, "I will speak to the one God who spawned all other gods, for I know him personally."

And Lyle J. French sayeth, "Only one god? That sounds doable."

And Joan Kearney didst seek out God, the original god, who now had tons of free time and was thinking about learning another language, maybe Italian.

And Joan Kearney sayest unto God, "The Industrialites wish to worship only you."

And God sayeth, "Only me? No other gods, not even Chuck, the god of peach pits?"

And Joan Kearney sayeth, "You alone."

And God sayeth, "I'm not in the god business anymore, plus I have tai chi classes."

And Joan Kearney sayest, "Thou can still take classes and be worshipped in name only, while the thousands of gods and goddesses who sprang from your loins keep things humming along."

And God sayest, "All right, what should I do?"

And Joan Kearney sayest, "Post a sign with your name only on every temple in the land. And also do a miracle once in a while, like appearing as a burning bush."

And God sayeth, "I shall have to clear that with Charlene, goddess of bushes."

And Joan Kearney sayeth, "All people will now believe there is only one true god, and although they don't know it, when they worship you they shall be in truth worshipping your many sons and daughters."

And God sayeth unto Joan Kearney, "Fine, let this be our little secret," then hurried off to his kitchen to try a new recipe for paella.

FRUGALITY MAY HURT NOW, BUT GIVE IT TWENTY YEARS

Folks who know me know I'm the kind of guy who likes to save a buck. That Dave Candish, they say, he gives tightfisted penny-pinching a good name.

So when I got promoted to a new job I said to my wife, Sally, "Let's not buy a big house. Let's live within our means. Let's save for a rainy day. Let's remember that money doesn't grow on trees, and a penny saved is a penny earned. . . ."

Sally had locked herself in the bathroom as per usual, but no problem, I would repeat my suggestions to her later that day, and again the next morning.

We bought an extremely modest home in spite of the six figures I earned as a supply-chain analyst. I was well paid because I loved my job. There wasn't a supply chain I didn't take pleasure in analyzing. I loved the long and short and medium-size chains, with their variety of interesting supplies, like beer nuts. But most of all I enjoyed building up our savings, the goal being to not spend money ever again.

I had our new life planned out. Eight-year-old Fiona and six-year-old Lucas could share a bedroom that doubled as an office for Sally, who was a part-time operations research analyst when she wasn't cleaning the house and buying groceries. I made furniture myself out of dumbbells and kettlebells, thus saving money on both home furnishings and gym memberships.

No way was I paying for an automobile either, not when my office was only seven miles away. I could stay in shape by walking it every morning while doing shoulder presses with an ottoman (kettlebell). And Sally stopped wasting money on groceries that weighed too much, knowing she'd be pushing the cart home along the side of the interstate.

One night everyone gathered around the dining room table (weight bench), and I shared more money-saving ideas:

"We don't need to take trips. We can tell each other horror stories about people on vacation having their organs harvested, so we can feel good about staying home with our kidneys intact.

"We don't need a pet. We can watch animal videos on free TV, once I get the coat hanger antenna to work. Come to think of it, we don't need TV. It'll be like somebody gave us a free coat hanger.

"We don't need toothpaste. After you brush, spit in a cup and save it and label your cup so we don't get confused about who owns which cup and which spit.

"BUT WHY?!" screamed Fiona and Lucas and, I'm ashamed to say, Sally.

"Because if we save money now we can enjoy it later."

"When?" said Fiona brightly. "Friday?"

"Friday in twenty years."

Fiona and Lucas melted onto the floor as if their spines had liquefied. I melted onto the floor too, in a display of good parenting.

"Hey kids. Remember the story of the ant and the grasshopper?"

"No," they said.

"Well, it's better to be an ant."

"Why?" they said.

They had me. I could only remember the moral—ants good, grasshoppers bad—and not the story itself. I tried winging it, saying ants were expert supply-chain analysts and grasshoppers pooped in their pants. Fiona and Lucas stared at me blankly.

I turned to Sally for moral support. Unfortunately she had also melted onto the floor and was now oozing in the direction of the bathroom door.

* * *

At the end of the month, as a result of my walk to work, I'd added two inches of lean muscle to my deltoids.

Sally wasn't doing as well. She was so exhausted after pushing the grocery cart home, she barely had the energy to analyze a single operation.

Worse than that, somehow we'd spent $34.72.

"Do you think we're made of money?" I said to Sally. I held a fistful of receipts, just like that Clint Eastwood western *A Fistful of Dollars*, probably released in Italy as *A Fistful of Receipts*.

"What are we supposed to do, Dave? We have to spend money to live."

"Name one," I said. One of what I wasn't sure, but it got her thinking.

"The kids' education," said Sally. "We need money for books and pencils and presentable clothes."

"Why don't we just burn our money on a big money bonfire?"

"Dave!"

Sally began to cry, and suddenly I felt guilty.

"I'm sorry. Good schooling is really important."

Then I had another inspired money-saving idea.

"Let's send the kids to the Death School," I said.

"The what?"

"The Death School. It's cheaper than other schools because of their no-frills education. I'm sure you've seen the bus driving around the neighborhood, the one that says Death Bus."

"That's horrible."

"Don't let the name put you off. If they didn't call it the Death School they'd be swamped with bargain hunters. The kids will be fine."

They were more than fine. Fiona and Lucas loved the Death School. They couldn't wait to come to terms with their own mortality each morning in homeroom.

The kids grew up happy and eventually healthy, after I taught myself pediatric medicine by trial and error.

Sally got tired of her trips to the supermarket, so she started her own garden. She grew vegetables that she'd sell to the neighbors at grossly inflated prices. Then we'd eat the weeds.

I kept getting promoted and winning awards, like Surplus Link Analyst of the Year. That wasn't my field, but I accepted the beautiful bronze award anyway, then sold it at a garage sale for a cool buck fifty.

And before we knew it we had saved a *lot* of money. We weren't prepared for a rainy day, we were prepared for years of rainy days, during which time the kids would grow old and die, an event they were mentally prepared for thanks to the Death School.

"Well, you did it," said Sally.

"We all did it," I told her. "We saved all our money, except for what we spent on medicine and a Crockpot for the weeds."

"Isn't it time to start spending?"

Spending.

"But wait . . . ," I spluttered. "We need to . . . a penny saved is a . . . a fool and his . . ."

The aphorisms that had sustained our family for years caught in my throat like sideways chicken bones. Three pairs of eyes stared at me, eyes that knew their time had come. After they had done without luxuries for so long, I had to admit I owed them.

"Okay. Let's"—the words emerged from my mouth like a slimy beast from hell—"spend money."

Lucas, now a grown man, was the first to go on a spree. He bought a new roll of duct tape to fix the shoes he'd been wearing since fifth grade. When he realized he could be more extravagant, he bought alligator shoes, then an alligator trench coat, and finally an alligator farm in St. Augustine, Florida, in case he thought of something else he wanted made out of alligator.

Unlike her brother, Fiona didn't start slow. Right out of the gate she bought dresses, jewelry, cars, houses. She spent money like a drunken sailor, and was made an honorary member of the Benevolent Order of Drunken Sailors.

I can't remember exactly when and where it hit me. It may have been when Sally and I were gazing at Central Park from our Fifth Avenue penthouse, or being served a seven-course meal by our personal chef at our villa in Saint-Tropez, or sipping spiced rum while sunbathing on our private beach in Antigua. One of those expensive places where furniture and gym equipment were two different things.

I turned to Sally, who now looked twenty years younger, and said, "Thanks to the sacrifices we made, we can now enjoy the best life has to offer. I embrace the abundance of the universe, not just materially, but mentally, emotionally, and spiritually. I love you."

I never felt worse.

CONCLUSIVE EVIDENCE

EXERCISE DETRIMENTAL TO YOUR HEALTH

A recent study has refuted previous claims that aerobic exercise promotes health. This study, performed over a three-day period by Dr. H. J. Chattergee and Dr. V. K. Chandra, both of the University of Michigan, proves conclusively that physical activity leads to disaster.

On Day One, the subjects of the study (Ed Huber of Frankfort, Illinois) were required to jog one mile. After fifty yards, the subjects (Ed) stumbled and fell headfirst onto the test track, receiving a minor concussion.

On Day Two, the subjects (Ed again) returned, and a heated argument with Drs. Chattergee and Chandra ensued. After being reminded he was being paid good money for the study, the subjects were shoved back onto the test track. This time, Ed stumbled after only six yards, receiving a second concussion on the other side of his head. The evidence was suggestive, but more testing was required.

On Day Three, Ed was hoisted out of his hospital bed by four orderlies and carried back to the track, where his legs were alternately lifted and planted in front of him by Drs. Chattergee and Chandra, in an attempt to simulate jogging. This time Ed traveled thirteen yards before collapsing onto the ground, screaming, "I hate science!"

Based on these results, aerobic exercise is not recommended; also not recommended is further study of aerobic exercise with Ed Huber.

* * *

EXCESSIVE ALCOHOL CONSUMPTION WILL NOT AFFECT YOUR ABILITY TO DRIVE A MOTOR VEHICLE

Drinking eight twelve-ounce beers before getting behind the wheel will have no effect on your reaction time, a recent study shows.

The subjects of the study (Ed Huber) consumed eight cans of beer during a twelve-minute period, afterward declaring, "Let's do some shots!" as foam dribbled down his chin. He was then escorted to his 2010 Chevy Malibu by Dr. S. P. Ramanujan of Stanford University, who reminded Ed that the study's budget covered only domestic beer, not Jameson Irish Whiskey.

Ed denied feeling any effects from the alcohol, explaining that his attempt to French kiss Dr. Ramanujan was because the doctor had rich full lips and didn't make him jog.

Assurances that he would not hit or run over anything were given by the subject before starting his car, sideswiping a dumpster, and flattening a chokeberry bush.

At the termination of his journey, in the driveway of Ed's home, an inspection of the front bumper revealed bits of mud, moss, ceramic tile, pizza dough, barbed wire, and animal fur. Ed asserted that these bits were there before he got in the car.

"Lesh do shome shots," Ed repeated, as his head dropped forward onto the steering wheel.

A control group (Ed's younger brother, Dave Huber) was pulled over and arrested after only five beers. Ed regained consciousness, declared "Dave's a lightweight," then vomited on the passenger seat.

* * *

Cause of Aging Pinpointed in Recent Study

New data now confirms the single greatest factor contributing to the aging process is talking on the phone to Janice.

All subjects (Ed) were monitored for seven common signs of aging, then compared with the control group (Dave).

Beginning in the opening seconds of the phone conversation ("What is it now, Janice?") and continuing for five minutes ("How many times do we have to go over this?"), wrinkles appeared on the subject's face at the rate of one every 3.4 seconds. Age spots on the hands appeared at the eight-minute mark ("You know what you are? You're a vampire."). After nineteen minutes ("Take the flat screen TV. See if I care."), the subject ended the conversation at the sudden onset of incontinence.

Dave, although not on the phone with Janice, displayed identical symptoms. He explained, "I was all the way in the next room and I could still hear them."

* * *

Studies Show It Is Possible to Become Smarter

You can easily boost you intelligence the way Ed Huber does by following the simple steps he described in a recent interview:

"Trust your instincts."

"Don't listen to scientists, even though they think they're so smart."

"Don't agree to do anything scientists ask you to do, even if they offer you money, because in the end it's more grief than it's worth."

"Don't read books, especially the ones written by know-it-all scientists."

"It's best not to read any books at all written by anybody, scientists or otherwise."

"If someone gives you a book as a gift, say, 'No thanks, I'm already smart.'"

"If you have a relative who's a scientist (I don't but maybe you do), don't invite them to Thanksgiving, because they will dominate dinner with their know-it-all science talk."

"Don't try to kiss scientists, because they'll only break your heart."

"Tell Dr. C. V. Rajneesh and Dr. S. P. Ramanujan to stop looking at me with those know-it-all faces and writing stuff in their notebooks."

* * *

Study Shows That Studies Are Unreliable

A recent scientific study proves that scientific studies prove nothing, especially when the subject is Ed Huber. This study of studies was conducted by Dave Huber, who revealed that Ed always had a real bad attitude toward scientists ever since he was a kid. Dave Huber proposed repeating the studies with himself as the subject, for more money. Dave insisted the results obtained would be reliable, and would also be a way to get back at Ed for all the swirlies he gave Dave in their toilet bowl back at the house.

THE MAN OF A TRILLION FACES

Before I give you my full report, let me clear something up: I really do have a trillion faces. Please don't ask to see them or we'll be here all night.

I'm aware I only show four faces on my website: one, me, Derek Organ, Private Investigator; two, me, Derek Organ, Private Investigator with a handlebar mustache; three, me, Derek Organ, Private Investigator with half a handlebar mustache and the other half pasted on my chin with spirit gum like a goatee; and four, the back of my head. I realize the back of my head is not technically a face, but still, I'm completely unrecognizable from that angle. Anyway, you wouldn't have hired me to shadow your wife if you weren't confident that I had a trillion faces.

And I don't need to tell you that having a trillion faces makes me a great people follower. What? I do need to tell you? Okay.

Here's how it works. Whenever the person I'm tracking suspects they're being followed, spins around, and sees me, I just change my face. If needed, I can do this a trillion times, though typically I tire after five and give up.

I'm glad you came to me and not the other Derek Organ online. He's not a private investigator. I think he's either a musician or my estranged father, who I haven't spoken with in twenty years.

Anyway, my report:

Using my current face, but with a handlebar mustache in my pocket just in case, I began tailing your wife. She was leaving her hair salon, and I can understand why you're worried she might be having an affair. She looked amazing. I seriously considered having an affair with her myself after I'd finished shadowing her and you'd paid me.

I followed her for several city blocks, doing a professional job of keeping my distance, except one time I got distracted by her sexy walk and realized my hands were on her hips like we were doing a conga line. I'm pretty sure she got a good look at my face before she slapped it. Then she flagged down a policeman and pointed me out. *Uh-oh*, I said to myself as I backed into an alley, *time to change into another of my trillion faces. Probably should pick one without a big red welt on the cheek.*

She ducked into a sexy lingerie shop in the Sexy Lingerie Shop District. This seemed a perfect time to disguise myself as a lingerie salesman. I had five thousand lingerie salesman faces to choose from, so I picked one with a pencil thin mustache, of which I had about two hundred.

I entered the shop and watched from a distance as she examined frilly nightgowns. Confident she wouldn't see through my disguise, I approached to try gathering more information.

"These nightgowns are very popular with women who are having affairs," I said.

"Is that a fact?" she said, eyeing my hands as if she suspected they had recently been on her hips.

"In fact, I think your lover would enjoy seeing you in this," I grabbed a black lace something off a rack and held it up. It was a teddy or a dish towel, I don't know, lingerie is not my field. She gave me a wary look, not one that said she recognized me, but rather one that said she's considering calling the cops.

"Zere is no need to worry," I assured her in a French accent I'd forgotten to use earlier. "I'm a professional lingerie salesman. If you'd like, I'll meet you in ze dressing room and help you try on your purchase, madame."

I dashed into the dressing room and waited. I probably should have let her go in first, but I was eager to see if my disguise was still effective in a confined space.

When she didn't appear for twenty minutes, I peeked out to find out what was keeping her.

She was nowhere in the store! I had wasted twenty minutes! I panicked for another ten minutes, then prepared to leave the lingerie shop and chase her. With spirit gum and my trusty handlebar mustache, I transformed into a mustachioed Olympic gold medal sprinter, a disguise that helped me run faster.

Back out on the street, I looked in both directions but didn't see her. I asked myself, if I were a woman having an affair, which way would I go? Clearly I would go someplace downhill from where I stood, because it was less work. I started running.

Then I spotted her. A woman! She looked nothing like your wife. She was a foot taller, wore denim overalls, and had massively overdeveloped forearms like Popeye.

It was then I realized I was dealing with a mistress of disguise. *She's a clever one*, I thought, *but a woman of a trillion faces can never fool a man of a trillion faces, as the saying goes.*

Oh, but she tried. As I shoved pedestrians out of the way in an effort to keep her in sight, she became a skinny supermodel, a feeble grandmother with a walker, a traffic cop, and a pear-shaped tourist from Minnesota. She used even more disguises in the next block.

I, in turn, transformed into a sidewalk Santa Claus, a two-year-old toddler, and a sexy lingerie salesman so I could practice my French accent.

And so, after a day of pursuing your wife, I can say with certainty she's having an affair. She is also selling arms to terrorists and will soon give a TED Talk on the Five Habits of Successful Entrepreneurs.

What do you mean, you're not going to pay me? You think I followed random strangers and made up a story about your wife being a mistress of disguise? As a professional investigator, I am deeply insulted.

Okay, pay me fifty percent. No? Then how about $5.95 for a bottle of spirit gum remover?

EVERYONE IS SO NICE, I JUST WISH I COULD SEE THEIR EYES

Mother and Father were normally reserved, but today at lunch they were in a state. Father, usually such a good eater, barely touched my prize-winning meat loaf.

"If you don't finish my prize-winning meat loaf, you won't get a slice of my prize-winning banana bread," I said, and then Mother began weeping and dropped to her hands and knees.

"Golly, I was just joshing," I said, as Father ripped the tablecloth to shreds.

For the first time since ever, my baby sister was missing a meal. She didn't answer the voice messages I left. Neither did she respond to the sounds of weeping and a ripping tablecloth that Mother and Father left.

"Golly, Mother and Father, it's no big whoop. Tiffy needs to spread her wings a little is all." I call her Tiffy for short. Her full name is Tiffany Upholstery, and I'm Mary Upholstery, and even though there's eight years between us, we could be identical twins except for I look older and less pretty.

"Don't be such worrywarts," I continued, but I don't think they heard me because now Father was breaking a juice glass so Mother could walk on the shards barefoot.

"Tell you what: I'll go through Tiffy's room for clues as to her whereabouts," I said, sounding like a detective or something.

In Tiffy's room I found a flyer that read, HELP WANTED AT THE GIANT PEANUT BUTTER COOKIE STORE. At first I thought that meant a big store for cookies, until I saw the picture on the flyer of a cookie next to a monster-truck tire, not nearly as big as the tire, but way bigger than a Chips Ahoy! Giant cookie store. I got it.

I read where the store was in Mainstreetville, USA. I'd heard of it. It was supposed to be a nice town, almost as nice as our town, Semen City, only with a nicer name.

I saw Tiffy's car keys on her vanity and deduced (detective!) that she had taken the train. I grabbed her keys, plus a framed picture of Tiffy, and headed for the front door.

I'm sure Mother and Father would have wished me luck, except they were painting COME HOME, TIFFANY on our roof in case she flew over in a helicopter.

I climbed into her Honda Civic and hit the road.

* * *

I wonder if this car is handling well, I thought as I drove down the interstate. I had never driven a Civic, and I had no idea what "handling well" meant. But golly, driving sure felt good. I'm embarrassed to admit it, but it was a relief to get away from Mother and Father. I loved them dearly, but life with them could be challenging, especially when they'd bitch-slap me for serving food that wasn't prize-winning. I thought, *What if I never came back? What if I kept driving and driving—* No, that's something Tiffy would do, not me.

TWENTY-FIVE MILES TO MAINSTREETVILLE, HOME OF THE GIANT PEANUT BUTTER COOKIE, the sign read.

My dear sister. She was the crazy one. Other than that, you couldn't tell us apart, aside from the age and prettiness differences I mentioned earlier. We were the same size and could exchange clothes. I was always happy to get her hand-me-downs. In fact, I had my eye on her brown low-heel closed-toe pumps, now that she'd graduated to brown mid-heel open-toe pumps. I told you she was crazy.

TEN MILES TO MAINSTREETVILLE, HOME OF THE GIANT PEANUT BUTTER COOKIE.

Peanut butter cookies started me thinking about treats. What if I got off at the rest stop ahead, used the ladies' facilities, and then went to the vending machine and bought some Twizzlers—no, that's something Tiffy would do, not me.

TAKE THE NEXT EXIT TO MAINSTREETVILLE, HOME OF—I couldn't read the next part of the sign because it had been painted over—AND ALSO THE GIANT PEANUT BUTTER COOKIE.

I took the exit.

* * *

Driving down Main Street in Mainstreetville, I thought, *Golly, this village is the definition of quaint.* Previously I thought Semen City was the definition of quaint. What did I know? The shops along the street were so cute and clean and perfect, you wanted to eat them, even the ones that weren't made of gingerbread.

The giant peanut butter cookie store stood at the end of the street, marked by a giant rotating giant peanut butter cookie sign. Hard to miss and rightly so, since this was the town's claim to fame. Oddly, there were no people on the sidewalk and no cars on the street. Great, I thought, more parking for me, and more cookies too. I parked under the spinning cookie and entered the shop.

The first thing that hit me was the marvelous aroma. It was that fresh-baked peanut-butter-cookie smell, coming from glass case after case of—you guessed it—fresh-baked giant peanut butter cookies. There was no one else in the shop.

"Hello?" I said, then rang a little bell.

A large middle-aged man emerged from the back, wiping peanut butter fingers on his apron.

"Howdy," he said, smiling broadly. "I'm Dan. Dan Doe. What can I do ya for?"

Dan's voice was so nice, and his smile so disarming, that it took me a moment to notice the black rectangular bar floating in the air in front of his face, hiding his eyes. I didn't mention it; I thought that would be rude. Maybe he couldn't help it. Maybe it was like a cold sore or something.

"Hi, Dan. I'm Mary."

"Pleased to meetcha. How many cookies you want?"

"Actually, I'm not here for cookies. I came to ask you a question."

"Fire away."

I retrieved the picture of Tiffy from my shoulder bag and handed it to him.

"This is my sister, Tiffany. She came here to apply for a job."

Dan gave the picture a close look. Apparently he could see right through that black bar; I guess it functioned like a floating one-way mirror.

"She's pretty . . ."

"I know."

"But not half as pretty as you."

I blushed. Did Dan wink at me? I couldn't tell.

"I'm awful sorry, Mary, but I've never seen her," he said, returning the picture to me.

"She never came here?"

"Nope. Sure you don't want a cookie?"

"I could go for a giant chocolate chip one."

"I only got peanut butter cookies. Yum." Dan licked his fingers.

"Giant chocolate chip cookies are very popular. If you started making those you might get more folks into your store." I gestured to the empty aisles.

Dan shrugged good-naturedly. "Aw, heck. I know business is slow, but it don't bother me." He leaned in close to my face. "I have other income streams," he said in a low voice, possibly winking again.

Then he straightened up. "You could ask across the way at the diner."

I guess I must've looked worried as I was biting my lip, because Dan said, "She'll turn up. Don't you worry."

I nodded, thinking how when someone with a black bar over their eyes says don't worry, it only makes you worry more.

* * *

The Mainstreetville Giant Peanut Butter Cookie Diner was quaint—do I even need to say that? Red-and-white-checked tablecloths. Little jukeboxes at every booth. Crusty yet lovable old waitress with curly red hair and a black bar over her eyes—oh, darn it.

Having had experience talking to a black-bar person, I approached her. Her name tag read, Greta Doe.

"Take a seat anywhere, hon," said Greta. Her niceness was undercut by the sound of her voice, electronically distorted, like she was gargling iron filings.

"You okay, hon?" More electric gargling. I pulled myself together and showed her Tiffy's picture.

"Have you seen my sister?"

"No, sorry, hon." Gargle. "Maybe one of the fellas over there saw her." Gargle gargle.

The fellas were four guys with black bars and plaid shirts, sitting in a booth drinking coffee. Bob Doe, Billy Doe, Buddy Doe, and Billy-Bob Doe couldn't have been nicer.

"Nope." Gargle.

"Sorry, haven't seen her." Gargle gargle.

"Just so you don't think we're lazy bums who have nothing better to do than hang out at the diner, you should know we have other income streams." One long gargle.

* * *

I ran down Main Street to the sheriff's office, easy to spot with its giant rotating cookie out front, cut in the shape of a star.

Bursting through the front door, I spotted the sheriff at his desk. Fortunately, he didn't have a black rectangle over his eyes—I don't think he did, anyway. It was hard to tell because his jacket was pulled up over his head.

"Howdy," he said in a muffled gargly voice. "And how are you this fine day?"

"Sheriff Doe," I said, reading his name tag, "I have no time for pleasantries. I need your help. My sister has gone missing, and I need you to find her."

I took the picture of Tiffy and stuffed it down the top of his jacket.

"Nope. Haven't seen her. Sorry." He returned the photo, then poured some coffee down the hole where his head should be.

"Then I need you go look for her." I was starting to get teed off.

"Aw, I'm sure she'll turn up eventually. Want a bite?" he offered, breaking off a piece of the peanut butter cookie that covered his entire desk.

"No, I don't want a bite!" I paced around the office, no longer charmed by its quaintness. "I'm beginning to think there's something strange going on around here. I believe folks should live and let live. But what with all the black bars I'm seeing and the weird voices I'm hearing, I'm starting to wonder if Tiffy is in danger."

From under the sheriff's jacket came a loud snore.

"Hey!" I slammed my fist on the desk, breaking the cookie in half.

"Huh?"

"Do something."

"Not now. I'm having dinner."

"You know something? You're a terrible sheriff."

"I know I'm terrible. Good thing I have other income streams."

* * *

Sick with worry, I hurried along Main Street, peering in shop windows, hoping to find Tiffy. But all I saw were black rectangles and smiles on the faces of the people of Mainstreetville who waved as I passed: the barber, the druggist, the dry cleaner. I stopped at the pet shop window and watched the puppies, wondering if, as the puppies grew, their little black rectangles would grow too.

"Psst."

Someone was pssting me.

"Where are you?" I said, looking around.

"In the alley."

The voice was barely a whisper, but at least it sounded natural, without electronic distortion. The alley was dark, dangerous, foreboding—and still somehow quaint.

"Step into the alley," the voice said. "Don't step on the old-timey charming rats."

I took cautious steps into the gloom.

"Who are you?"

"Never mind who I am." The voice seemed to be coming from one of a dozen garbage cans.

"*Where* are you?"

"Never mind that either. I know where your sister is."

"*Where?*"

"That information doesn't come free," said a brick wall.

"You want cash? I'll give you everything I have."

"What I want is a giant chocolate chip cookie. I'm sick of peanut butter."

"I could make a prize-winning giant chocolate chip cookie," I said breathlessly. "After I find Tiffy I'll mail it to you."

"It's a deal. Send it to Mainstreetville, care of the Dark Alley," said the brick wall.

"Actually, I'd prefer oatmeal raisin." The voice came from down around my feet.

"Oatmeal, yuck," said a new voice from the garbage can. "Make it a caramel pecan snickerdoodle."

"I'll make you as many cookies as you want. Just tell me where Tiffy is."

The voices became even quieter—the garbage can, the brick wall, and what I now realized was a rat.

"She's at the Mainstreetville Movie Studio," said the garbage can.

"Whatever you do, don't say we sent you there," said the brick wall.

"Our cookie preferences could put the lives of our families in danger," said the rat.

"I'll be discreet," I told them. "And I think your disguises are really good."

"I could go for some lemon squares," said an old fire escape.

* * *

I found the side door to the Mainstreetville Movie Studio, marked by a flashing red light and a sign that read, FILMING IN PROGRESS: NO SNEAKING IN. I sneaked in.

Crouching in the darkness, I watched a whirlwind of activity. Greta the waitress stood behind a camera, twirling knobs. The four fellas from the diner booth moved lights around. Dan from the cookie store was doing deep knee bends. He wore his cookie apron and nothing else.

All the attention was centered around what I first thought was a round bed made to look like a peanut butter cookie. Then I realized it was an actual peanut butter cookie the size of a round bed.

In vain I looked for Tiffy amid the stagehands, technicians, costume, makeup, and hair people. My search was made even more difficult by the fact that, in addition to the black rectangles that covered everyone's eyes, their bodies were hidden by vibrating blurry squares.

"Tiffy!" I cried.

"Mary!" I thought I heard a gargly response. But I couldn't tell from where. I frantically pushed my way through the movie crew.

Then I saw them. The only parts of Tiffy that weren't vibrating and blurry.

Brown mid-heel open-toe pumps. I ran to them.

I felt around above the shoes, found her hand, and grabbed it.

"Let's go, Tiffy."

We ran for the side entrance, blocked by the blurry image of Sheriff Doe, his jacket still covering his head.

We knocked him to the floor, gave him a few brutal kicks, and dashed out of the studio.

"Told you I was a terrible sheriff," he said from inside his jacket.

* * *

In the car driving home, Tiffy said, "They told me it was part of the training to become a giant-cookie salesperson. You wouldn't believe the things they wanted to film me doing."

"I don't need to hear about them."

"I was so naive."

"None of that is important. What's important is getting you back home safely to Mother and Father and Semen City."

"Back to normalcy," she said.

We drove in silence for several miles.

"Tiffy . . . do you mind if I . . . would it be all right . . . ?"

"You want to try on the rectangular bar?"

"If you wouldn't mind."

She passed me her black bar and I put it in front of my eyes. Like every other hand-me-down Tiffy ever gave me, it fit perfectly.

I began to get ideas.

Golly.

THAT'S WHAT FISTS ARE FOR

A book can change your life. I want to share with you the tale of my personal transformation, the result of reading a book and then punching people.

My name is Henry Maraschino, like the cherry, and I work, or used to work, in customer service at Lippmann Reynolds, the upscale department store. I specialized in answering questions about ladies' accessories, like "Where are ladies' accessories?" "Do you carry ladies' accessories?" and sometimes, "Ladies' accessories?" My response to all these questions would be the same: "Second floor," I would say, as I made an upwardly directed gesture with my right index finger (I am right-handed).

My expertise vis-à-vis the location of ladies' accessories was such that I was not confined to a position behind a counter but rather roamed freely about the floor as a sort of traveling information maven. I dressed appropriately, wearing a charcoal gray suit with a red carnation in my lapel, picked fresh daily, and an Eton silk tie, also picked fresh daily.

I'm embarrassed to admit, if I were asked about anything other than ladies' accessories, I was at sea. I would do my best to answer questions like "Where are men's accessories?" or "You're a preening little cream puff, aren't you?" ("Third floor, maybe" and "I suppose I am.") But these less-than-satisfactory exchanges left me feeling painfully incompetent. I knew better than to display my frustration at work, so when my shift ended, I'd hurry homeward. After changing out of my Eton answer-questions-about-ladies'-accessories silk tie and into my Eton punch-myself-in-the-face silk tie, I would punch myself in the face. I was able to spare my visage serious harm by using a pair of slightly damaged boxing gloves, obtained at no charge from the sporting goods department, one of the many perks of working at Lippmann Reynolds.

Afterward, with my frustration adequately expressed, I slept soundly, after first placing an Egyptian cotton bath towel on my pillow to prevent bloodstains.

As a result of my self-battering, my right hook grew powerful. I would bob and weave, but there was no escaping my own knuckle sandwich.

With the holiday season upon us, a massive throng of customers bombarded me with questions, few of which were, sadly, related to ladies' accessories. As Christmas grew closer, my feelings of inadequacy increased. You could see the story of my nightly self-reproof writ large on my countenance.

One day, my boss, Mr. Matthews, whose small round head came no higher than my carnation, drew me aside.

"Maraschino, what gives? Your nose is broken, your lips are swollen, you're missing a couple front teeth, and your eyes are giant plums."

"I have an abusive spouse," I said, making light of the situation.

"You're not married."

"I fell down the stairs."

"You live on the ground floor."

He was a shrewd one.

"I should fire you. You're a disgrace to Lippmann Reynolds."

My hands balled into fists. I wished I was back in my apartment where I could teach myself a lesson.

"Go home and stay there," growled Matthews. "And slap a pair of beefsteaks on those peepers."

Free meat from the gourmet food shop was another perk of working at Lippmann Reynolds, provided the gratis steaks were week-old and had little rainbows on them.

That evening, my efforts to smack myself were frustrated by the beefsteaks, which kept sliding down my cheeks and onto the floor. In frustration I collapsed on the sofa and reached for my mobile phone, thinking mindless exploration of clickbait sites might distract me from my distress. After removing my boxing gloves and clicking on the enticing link, "These Famous Celebrities Forgot to Wear Pants," I saw a banner ad at the bottom of the page that seemed to speak directly to me:

IT'S TIME TO STOP PUNCHING YOURSELF IN THE FACE.

After forwarding $97, I received the life-changing e-book I mentioned earlier, titled simply *Choice*. I will summarize it:

We have no control over what happens to us. But we can control our reaction. We can choose our response.

The book made the same point over and over for two hundred pages. Despite the needless repetition, it had a profound effect on me. Punching myself was the response I had chosen. But could I choose another?

At that moment, rather than striking myself for spending $97, not exactly a waste but not exactly a bargain either, I chose differently. I chose to punch my phone. Which I did. I punched it across the room. And I felt exhilarated.

Then I made another choice. I chose to obey a voice in my head telling me to wear boxing gloves to work.

"I told you to stay home," said Matthews, glowering up at me. "I oughta fire you."

It worked on my phone. Let's try it on a person.

"I choose to punch you," I said to Matthews, then delivered a right hook to his jaw that sent him skidding across the floor.

Mr. Matthews was exponentially larger than a cell phone, likewise was the thrill I got from laying him low.

Again, my choice was not right or wrong. It was just a choice, one I looked forward to making again soon.

"What do you mean you don't know where children's clothing is?"

POW. A jab sent the young mother stumbling backward into a display of winter hats.

"What's with the boxing gloves, fruitcake?"

BAM. A left uppercut made the young punk spin like a top.

"Where's the bathroom?"

"I'm sorry, ma'am, but if I don't hit you, I'll end up going home and hitting myself."

"I understand completely, young man."

WHUMP WHUMP WHUMP. A series of body blows to the old woman's torso.

Not right or wrong. Just choices.

"I'm choosing new responses," I explained to Matthews and Matthews's boss and Matthews's boss's boss in whose office we had gathered. The two higher-ups stood there, frowning. Matthews cowered in the corner, protecting himself with a damaged umbrella he'd gotten free from men's accessories, another perk of working at Lippmann Reynolds.

"You're fired," said Matthews's boss's boss. Matthews's boss repeated, "Fired." Matthews wrote the word "fired" in the air with the tip of his crooked umbrella.

I was told to leave the building immediately.

On my way out I swung my fists madly, knocking the heads off mannequins and the hats off security guards.

A new world opened up for me. At home I recklessly knotted my tie in a new way. No more half-Windsors for me. Now it was a full-Windsor or nothing.

I was determined to make up for the occasions when I didn't think I could choose my response. Where better to start than good old Thomas Edison High, where I had been mercilessly bullied. It was time for retribution. I punched out a homeroom teacher and stole a hall pass. Then I roamed the halls, using my fists on anybody I saw bullying anybody else, or anybody who looked like they might bully somebody else, or anybody I felt like bullying myself, just to walk a mile in the shoes of a bully.

The principal expelled me. I decked him, cleaned out some kid's locker since I didn't have a locker of my own, and departed.

Unfortunately, over time, my adrenaline high began to lessen. Even worse, my boxing gloves had worn out and were now mere bits of ragged padding dangling from my perspiring hands.

I reread my copy of *Choice* or, rather, reread the first paragraph, which covered everything.

We can choose our response.

Say! I had been so focused on responding to people with punches, I forgot I could also kick them.

At that moment I missed my free Lippmann Reynolds perks, which might have included a pair of steel-toe boots from the men's shoe department.

No matter. I bought a pair of steel-toe boots with my own money, figuring the boots would one day pay for themselves.

Hitting the streets, ready to kick ass, and I mean literally someone's physical ass, I hoped to engage someone in polite conversation, and then as they turned to walk away:

KICK KICK KICK (ass-kicking sound).

This was satisfying, and at the same time frustrating. All I could manage were back-of-the-ankle kicks because my hamstrings were stiff. I acquired a new respect for professional dancers, who I'm sure could kick someone in the ass with ease.

In order to gain greater flexibility, I enrolled in a beginning ballet class. Every Saturday morning, I did pliés and jetés with nine-year-old girls in pink tutus. Then after class I would tell them that if they persisted with their training, a whole world of ass-kicking would open up to them.

By tiny degrees, my flexibility improved. But it's funny. Even before I hit the streets with my steel toes and my supple limbs, the thrill of kicking began to lose its glamour, same as punching.

I sat on my sofa, ruminating.

We can choose our response.

Punching, kicking. Was there yet another response?

Nothing came to mind. I resolved to keep thinking about it.

In the meantime I needed money. The steel-toe boots had set me back a pretty penny.

I applied for a job at the Ultimate Fighting Federation.

"What are your qualifications?" said Lars, the shirtless, heavily tattooed fighter sitting behind a desk and reviewing my application.

"I can punch, kick, and direct people to ladies' accessories," I said, pointing upward with my right index finger.

"Okay," said Lars. "We'll give you a test match. You'll face Igor 'the Tibia Breaker' Kalashnik. He prefers tibias, but he'll settle for any bone that's handy."

It wasn't a fair fight. During the first few seconds I weakened him with a flurry of punches and kicks. But it was a jab from my upwardly directed right index finger that finished him off.

And that's how I became Henry "Cherry Boy" Maraschino, the baddest, fiercest fighter on the UFC circuit. I make millions per year. The days of roast beef rainbows are far behind me.

One evening, as I iced my right index finger, I picked up my phone and took another peek at *Choice*. Somehow I had overlooked the appendix:

When in a state of upset, the best choice one can make is to find serenity by taking long, slow, deep breaths.

I punched my phone across the room.

THE PEOPLE OF THE TEMPORARY TATTOO

Did they exist? Or were they the stuff of legend, a fairy story parents told their children to make them think twice about body art? I would soon learn the truth. I would soon come face-to-face with the People of the Temporary Tattoo.

My name is Tyler Cruikshank. I'm a journalist and explorer, drawn to the fringes of human experience, provided the plane trip isn't too long and I'm in business class.

One day, I was called into a meeting with Avery Totz, publisher of *Couch Potato Voyager Magazine*.

"Cruikshank," said Totz from behind his leopard-skin desk, "I was impressed by your article in *Couch Potato Globe-Trotter Monthly*."

"The one about the Inuit in the prefab igloos."

"Yep. You're just the man to write about the P.O.T.T.T."

Counting the T's, I realized he meant the People of the Temporary Tattoo.

"I want you to travel to the Amazon rain forest and find them."

I'd heard of journalists who had gone in search of the P.O.T.T.T. and never returned. I'd also heard of the Amazon rain forest, the most dangerous forest in the world.

I rose from the hippo-shaped love seat. "Nice talking with you, Totz."

"Please reconsider. We pay generously." He wrote a figure on a Post-it note shaped like a banana leaf and passed it to me.

"I need to fly business class," I said.

"If you find the tribe, you'll make history."

"And don't book me in an exit row and tell me the leg room is the same, because it isn't."

We shook hands and drank coconut LaCroix from plastic shells. Tyler Cruikshank was on the job.

After a hellish nine-hour flight, during which the sound in the left ear of my individual headset was distorted, we landed in São Paulo. My plan was to fly to Manaus, enter the rain forest, find the tribe, say hello, then hit Totz up for an upgrade from Business to First.

Somehow I made it through the next two-hour flight without freshly baked chocolate chip cookies. I arrived shaken but alive in Manaus.

"People of the Temporary Tattoo?" I didn't speak the native tongue, so I posed my question to passers-by using universal sign language. They responded with universal derisive laughter.

"People of the Temporary Tattoo?" I asked humble peasants on the fringes of the jungle. They threw fistfuls of mud at me, until I taught them how to laugh derisively, which they did while continuing to throw mud.

Sitting by the side of the wet road, despondent, ready to abandon my quest, I became aware of a green anaconda encircling my torso. *I'm a goner*, I thought.

The snake gave me a look that said, *People of the Temporary Tattoo? Follow me.*

* * *

The snake knew its way around the rain forest, no surprise there. I figured if I wanted to survive I should mimic it, so I slithered along the ground and, for dinner, would swallow a whole capybara after crushing it with my powerful coils (thighs).

I found slithering and swallowing giant rodents to be a pleasant distraction. Before long the airplane cookie fiasco was forgotten. Nevertheless I began to despair, thinking I would never find the missing tribe. My anaconda guide gave me a look that said, *Be patient.* The Matrix *was a great film, but* Matrix II *and* Matrix III *sucked really hard.* At that point I was probably hallucinating.

One day as I lay on the jungle floor digesting a peccary, my ears were treated to an enchanting sound, a female voice singing a song I would later learn was called "Bathing in the Lagoon." I drew aside some ferns, peered through, and beheld a naked young woman, bathing in the lagoon.

The anaconda gave me a look that said, *I'd wink if I had eyelids,* then discreetly slipped away.

I turned back to the young woman, and that's when I saw it, on her left upper arm: a henna tattoo, blurry and faded.

I burst through the ferns and ran to the edge of the lagoon. She screamed.

"Please don't be afraid," I said, "I won't—*BURP*, peccary, excuse me—I won't harm you."

She stopped screaming. I pointed to myself.

"Me—Tyler."

"Me—Debi."

She stood there waist-deep, with an innocent smile, unashamed of her nakedness. There was another faded tattoo over her left breast that read *nor*.

Her garment was at my feet, a sarong or a tank top or a muumuu, who can remember the names of women's clothing? I held it out as she emerged from the lagoon.

I didn't want to build my hopes up, but I had a feeling Debi could lead me to the People of the Temporary Tattoo, or at least to the tattoo store where they shopped.

From the start Debi and I shared an easy rapport. Her English was surprisingly good, having learned it from other travel writers.

"Can you take me to the People of the Temporary Tattoo?"

She nodded. "My tribe."

Bingo.

We walked side by side through the jungle.

"Debi, I noticed earlier you have a tattoo that says nor."

She nodded. "My boyfriend. He is called Ron."

"The tattoo is backward."

"I am told it looks better in a mirror. One day I hope to have a mirror."

"But why is it backward?"

"It is a chance we take with temporary tattoos. It has been so since the world began."

She stopped and placed a hand on my arm.

"Now you must show me your tattoos."

"I don't have any."

Debi laughed. "Silly white man. Come on, show me."

Before I knew it she had unbuttoned my shirt and pulled it off.

She gasped and touched my chest. "White skin like a cloudless sky. No tattoos, not even hair."

"I'm one-sixteenth Cherokee."

"Ron has hair. All the time he talks about his hair and his long penis. He bores me."

With that Debi threw her arms around my neck, pressed her body against mine, and gave me a long, lovely kiss. She tasted of peccary. Wish I'd brushed my teeth. Still it was thrilling.

She released me. "Here is our village."

In the clearing in the middle of the settlement, women pounded grain to make flour and small children played tag. Every villager displayed indistinct tattoos on their arms and legs. I was transported back to a simpler time, a time before cell phones and permanent huts; these huts were wobbly and slapdash.

"And this is your home?" I said.

"Only for the next one to two months, until our tattoos have completely faded."

"Have you ever considered getting permanent tattoos?"

She laughed. "No, foolish white man. If we did that, we wouldn't live in half-finished huts."

I nodded respectfully. Their culture was old, older than logic itself.

Debi pulled me forward.

"Attention, everyone! This is Tyler. He wants to write about us before he perishes in the rain forest like the others. He has no tattoos."

The women and children gathered around me, pulling off my shirt, oohing and aahing.

"Debi, where are the men?" I said.

"They will be returning soon. In the morning hours they do temp work."

It wasn't long before the men arrived, walking single file, led by a tall boisterous youth with more blurry tattoos than the others. He even had tattoos on his face, including one on his forehead that said IBED.

"I hate shaving my body hair," he announced to his companions as he strode along, "but when I do it makes the tattoos stay on better, especially in the area around my long penis."

Ron froze when he saw me with my shirt off, standing by Debi.

"I do not like this stranger," he said, advancing on me.

Ron shoved Debi aside and glared at me.

"Debi is *my* woman. See?" He pointed to the tattoo on his forehead.

"IBED?"

"I am told it looks better in a mirror."

I felt bold, having been seduced by Debi's kiss. I longed to put this rain forest punk in his place.

"It's a good thing her name will soon fade from your forehead," I sneered, "because she wants nothing to more to do with you."

Ron balled up his fists. "I want to pound your body so hard that instead of tattoos, you'll have bruises that last even longer than one to two months."

"Bring it," I said, for the first time in my life.

"Enough!" croaked a feeble commanding voice. The villagers fell silent. An old man emerged from one of the unfinished huts, his skin blue from decades of faded tats.

"That is Fred, our tribal leader," Debi whispered to me.

The villagers parted to allow Fred through. He stepped between me and Ron.

"There shall be a duel," he proclaimed. "The winner will take this woman."

"Hey!" I said. "You can't talk about her like she's a piece of property."

"Why not?" said Debi.

"Well . . . if you're okay with it . . ."

We were each given a big stick, then placed at opposite sides of the clearing. At a signal, we were to charge into the center and beat each other until one of us collapsed.

"This stick is thicker than my penis," said Ron, "but not as long."

"Please don't talk, just fight," I said.

Fred gave the signal. Ron and I charged each other. When he got halfway to the center, Ron seemed to lose interest. He stopped, tore a piece of bark off his stick, and used it to comb the hairs on his forearm.

As per tradition, if you're in a duel and you lose interest last, you're declared the winner and made an honorary member of the tribe.

That night, while everyone chanted and feasted on half-baked chicken, Fred made me remove my shirt. He then applied a full-arm temporary tattoo. It was either a dragon or a samurai warrior. He put it on crooked, it only covered two thirds of my arm, and it itched.

I was the first white man to join the People of the Temporary Tattoo. Or so I thought.

Ron took his defeat well. He scratched the letter T on his forehead, then went looking for a girl named debit.

I moved into Debi's shabby hut, and we settled into a comfortable daily routine. Every morning she bathed in the lagoon, singing "Bathing in the Lagoon," and I went with the men to do temp work. At night we ate half-cooked plantains with the rest of the tribe. Whenever I suggested we cook our food all the way, insults were hurled at me, like "be quiet, fully-cooked-food-eating white man!"

In honor of our love, I gave myself a tattoo on my forearm with a sharp stick and acai berry juice. It said debi. I thought she'd love it because it was permanent and she didn't have to read it backward. She smiled when she saw it, but her smile held a secret.

I loved my new life with Debi. Little did I know we had few precious moments left.

One night as we lay in our hut, rain pouring in through the half-finished roof, I asked, "Would you ever get a tattoo of my name—RELYT—on your breast?"

"Maybe tomorrow. Go to sleep," she said.

I tried to sleep, and eventually drifted off, dreaming of Debi and peccaries and backward names.

In a half-awake state, I felt the rain pouring on me, twice as hard.

Twice as hard.

No!

I opened my eyes. There was no longer half a leaky roof sheltering me. There was no roof at all. There was no Debi. There was no village.

While I slept, they'd departed. They didn't tell me, and it wasn't because they forgot. They were offended I'd given myself a permanent tattoo, in defiance of their tradition.

I knew this day was coming. Debi told me they'd be leaving. She said according to custom, they must follow the elder Fred to the rain forest Party City, where he would trade guavas for more tattoos. A lottery would determine who got what. Debi had been lucky when she drew henna ink, but she lived in fear of one day getting Yosemite Sam.

Knowing better than to try to follow a tribe that no longer wanted me, I wandered through the dense undergrowth. Lost, desolate, I knew I would soon perish.

Delirious from hunger, I collapsed onto the jungle floor.

I was revived by the appetizing and somewhat familiar odor of roasting meat.

"Snake kebabs," a voice said. Next to me on a spit, rotating over an open flame, was my old friend the anaconda guide. A look in its eyes said—well, nothing really, it was dead. My poor snake buddy. I was given a skewer with a side of lemon rice, and my grief gave way to lip-smacking satisfaction.

As I ate, the six men watching me came into focus. With their tattered Orvis safari shirts, they were unmistakably the missing travel writers.

"Look," said one writer in a shredded panama hat, pointing to my forearm, "He has the mark of ibed. Only it's backward."

"If our IBED tattoos have faded away," said another writer touching his forehead, "he shouldn't have one either."

They held me down and spent twenty minutes scraping and scouring my forearm, to no avail. The acai berry ink was permanent.

"It won't come out," Panama Hat declared. "He must be a god."

They knelt before me. The jungle had made them crazy.

And that's how I came to be the leader of my own tribe, The People Who Sought the People of the Temporary Tattoo. During the day we forage for food. At night we sit around the fire telling Debi stories. Then we sing a slow, sad version of "Bathing in the Lagoon."

I'm placing these pages in a Pellegrino bottle, dropping in into the mighty Amazon, and hoping it will be carried to the sea. If you find it, please take it to Avery Totz at *Couch Potato Voyager Magazine*. Collect my fee and hold it for me. I swear I will return.

Probably in one to two months.

MY YEAR WITH THE PERFECT FAMILY

Day One

I gunned down the mother and the daughter in their respective beds. When the son came out of his bedroom I shot him in the hallway. And when the father came home late from work I stabbed him to death at the front door.

* * *

Day Two

Hm. That may have been a mistake.

My name is Davis Barnes and I'm a documentary filmmaker. I'd already been paid half of my five thousand dollar fee to make "My Year with the Perfect Family," for the Perfect Family Network. I was excited at the prospect of spending a year with a family so unlike my own.

Now the subjects of my documentary were dead, and I had 364 days to go before I got the rest of my money.

I sat down on the living room sofa. I filmed a few seconds of the father, crumpled in a bloody heap at the front door. I didn't need a crew. I was shooting the doc on my phone using the DocumentaryPro app, and while it was a versatile app, it still couldn't make a dead guy who didn't move look interesting.

I put my phone down and thought about my situation.

* * *

DAY THREE

Got a call from Norman Spleen, the Executive Director of the Perfect Family Network. He wondered how things were going with the perfect family. I said I murdered them. He laughed. I said, no, I'm serious, I murdered them. He laughed again. I said I really really murdered them. He said, okay, take it easy, and hung up.

I was glad I could brighten his day.

* * *

DAY FOUR

Still on the sofa. Still thinking.

As a documentary filmmaker I'd seen my share of ugliness. I reflected on my previous work:

My Year in a War Zone. My first documentary. It was ugly and loud.

My Year Riding to Fires in a Fire Engine. Also ugly, with the burning buildings, and also loud, with the siren.

My Year with Rabid Dogs. Even though the dogs were good-looking, they tried to bite me all the time, which to me made them ugly.

My Year Locked in a Closet with an Ugly Eighty-Nine-Year-Old Woman Suffering from Halitosis. That film won all kinds of awards. People responded to the intimacy. Unfortunately it didn't make a dime.

It was an impressive body of work, but it was all negative. It was time to make a film that captured the best of humanity and affirmed wholesome family values.

I shot a few more seconds of the father's rotting corpse.

* * *

Day Five

Still thinking.

This time, instead of being in my film, I wanted to be a fly on the wall. I wanted my subjects to forget I was there, which I guess they did, which was why it was so easy to kill them.

Why did I do it?

The easy answer is, because they were *too* perfect. And you know what? The easy answer is the right answer. I mean, come on.

They said "good morning" and "good night."

They said "please" and "thank you."

The son and daughter were straight B students. They could have been straight A students, but they didn't want to make their classmates feel bad by being too perfect, which was another perfect thing about them, which is why I killed them.

* * *

Day Six

They flossed three times a day.

They wiped their feet when they came in the front door. If the father had spent a little less time wiping his feet, he might've seen me coming with the knife.

I approached them when I saw them patiently waiting at an intersection for the WALK light. They said they'd do the documentary, not so they could be on TV just to be famous, but so they could help people everywhere feel better about themselves.

"Wish I could say I felt better," I said to the dead dad.

* * *

DAY SEVEN

I thought I should stare at the other dead family members for a while. But I liked the sofa. It was comfortable. So I dragged it upstairs.

* * *

DAY TWENTY-TWO

(I'm skipping the days when I left the house and stayed at a hotel, because, man, that smell. Made me miss the old lady with halitosis.)

So I'm back in the house now, having gotten some nice footage of the breakfast buffet at the Holiday Inn Express.

Norman Spleen left a voice mail message saying that the joke about murdering the family was really good, but now he needs to see some film.

I left him a message saying would he like to see footage of their bloody bodies, hoping to get a wee bit more mileage out of the gag.

Maybe I have a problem with the concept of perfection. What is perfection anyway? Different people have different ideas about perfection. To some people, perfection is a family that's considerate and kind. To others perfection is dead bodies sprawled around a nice house. I need to develop this thought further, for when they catch me.

* * *

DAY TWENTY-FIVE

I've wasted enough time pondering perfection. Time to get busy doing what I've been paid to do.

Where to begin? Air freshener.

* * *

Day Twenty-seven

Bought about five hundred of those little pine tree air fresheners and hung them around the house like I saw in the movie *Seven*.

I need to pose the stiff bodies in domestic scenes and then film them.

Shouldn't be too tough.

I need to move their hands and arms around a little.

Tricky, but I can handle it.

Plus I need to do all their voices.

This is impossible. I give up.

* * *

Day Twenty-eight

Got a call from Norman Spleen, demanding to see footage of the family, and I said, "How about footage of dried blood on the carpet?" and he said, "The time for levity is over."

Spleen said if I didn't send him something in the next forty-eight hours I would never see the rest of my money.

* * *

Day Twenty-nine

"For this food we are about to eat, we are grateful," said Dad with his head bowed and me crouched down behind him, holding his hair. Then I lifted him up, careful not to accidentally snap his head off his body.

I thought saying grace was a nice "perfect" touch. I'd placed Dad at the head of the table, and then applied makeup to everyone, which helped a little bit—although I also planned for everyone to say to each other, "You don't look well," because I'm bad at makeup.

In addition to complimenting Mom on the her perfect turkey dinner, and Mom blushing (tomato paste), I thought I'd have the kids talk about their day at school, and how they almost got A's until they remembered to get B's to make their classmates happy. I wanted them to sing a song in four-part harmony about how important it was to make others happy, but I'm also bad at ventriloquism.

These were my plans. But all I really managed to shoot was Dad saying grace, then falling face first into his mashed potatoes.

I sent twenty-two seconds of film to Norman Spleen.

* * *

DAY THIRTY-ONE

I'm in a panic. Norman Spleen and several executives from the Perfect Family Network liked the twenty-two seconds I sent and are going to pay me a visit. They want to meet the family in person.

I said, "Don't come, the family is sick."

They said they could see they were sick. But they had to meet a family where the father said grace while the family sat there so quiet and respectful.

What was I going to do?

I know! I will say the family left on a family vacation in the family car to a family destination. A Disney something-or-other park. And they decided to take me with them, once they remembered I was there, since I was doing such a good job being a fly on the wall.

I would put the family in the car and drive it around the corner, out of sight. Then I would fly to some Disney something-or-other park and buy postcards and mail them to Norman Spleen. "Greetings, Norman. Signed (their names)."

Note to self: find out their names.

Once I'd formed my plan, I no longer felt panicked. I sat on the sofa and reflected one last time on the nature of perfection before I fell asleep.

* * *

DAY THIRTY-TWO

Bang! Bang! Bang!

I jumped three feet in the air when I heard pounding outside the house.

Workmen were boarding up the windows!

I ran to the front door and threw it open.

Norman Spleen was standing there with a bunch of guys in suits I didn't recognize.

"Good morning, Davis."

"Good morning, Mr. Spleen."

Norman Spleen gestured to the guys behind him.

"I showed your twenty-two seconds of film to them and they were impressed."

"Are they with the Perfect Family Network?"

"No, they're with the Ghost Family Network."

"Ah," I said, trying to grasp the big picture and failing.

"I've sold your project to them. From now on it will be called My Year with the Ghost Family."

"So I get paid double?"

"No, you don't get paid anything. You violated our contract when you murdered the family."

"That must have been in the fine print. And — hey! Who says I murdered them?"

"Come on, Davis. It was obvious from the footage they were dead."

A toothy young executive stepped forward.

"Hi, Davis. Bart Withers, Ghost Family Network. We're looking very much forward to working with you. We're boarding you up in the house with the dead family. You'll shoot footage of their ghosts. At the end of a year, I'm confident we'll have a terrific product. I'm very excited."

The other toothy young executives nodded, indicating that they too were very excited.

"And what if I don't want to do it?" I said.

"Uh . . ." The Ghost Family Network executives stood there in confused silence.

"I'm pulling your legs," I said. "Of course I want to do it. I'm very excited too."

The young toothy executives smiled toothy smiles.

"See you in a little less than a year," I said as I went back in the house.

* * *

DAY TWO HUNDRED SEVENTY-NINE

"For this food we are about to eat, we are grateful," hissed Ghost Dad.

"Amen," hissed Ghost Mom, Ghost Son, and Ghost Daughter, raising their heads.

"That's a keeper," I said as I filmed the family from the far end of the table. Thankfully, their physical bodies lay rotting and stinking in the basement. Only their ghost bodies remained at the table.

"Unfortunately, the light wasn't quite right. Can we do one more?"

"Of course," said Ghost Dad.

"We'd be glad to," said Ghost Son.

"We'll do as many as you want, Davis," said Ghost Daughter.

"We'll do whatever makes you happy," said Ghost Mom.

"Guys, all you have to be now are ghosts," I told them. "You don't have to be perfect anymore."

"Okay," they said, but they couldn't help it. They couldn't help being perfect.

I would have killed them again if they weren't already dead.

THE HUGGING DETECTIVE

I was sitting at my desk the way a private detective was supposed to sit, with my feet up, my fedora cocked rakishly to one side, and half a bottle of cheap Scotch in the bottom drawer. Okay, full disclosure: Business had been bad lately and I'd been forced to sell my desk. The bottle was on the floor, and when I put my feet up, there was nothing to rest them on. My leg cramps made me want to scream.

I was leaning forward, rubbing my hamstrings to get the circulation back, when she walked in on a pair of gams in fishnet stocking, gams that had to be illegal in all fifty-seven states and the twelve U.S. territories. I thought it best to maintain my self-control, so I continued rubbing my hammies and hoped she wouldn't think I was masturbating. The thought of running my eyes up her anatomy to behold the rest of her thrilled me, like opening anatomy-shaped presents on Christmas morning.

"Mr. Organ?"

"That's me. Derek Organ, private detective."

"My name is Harriet Devereaux."

Her name had a lot of syllables, eight or nine by my count, almost as many as U.S. territories. I wish it had more syllables because every time she uttered one, I could feel her warm breath on the back of my neck.

I decided it was time to look up.

"Don't feel you have to put your feet down on my account," she said, as my legs flailed helplessly in the air.

"Scotch, Ms. Devereaux?" I offered, kicking over the bottle.

"The drawer I usually keep in is at the cleaners," I lied.

"Let's get right to the point, Mr. Organ."

She squatted down a little and pretended to sit in a chair that wasn't there. I guess she didn't want to hurt my feelings.

"My ex-husband was just released from prison."

"What did he do time for?"

"Robbing a candy store. For me. I have a sweet tooth."

"I bet you do, with those gams."

"What's that supposed to mean?"

"Nothing, Ms. Devereaux. What brought you here?"

"I'm afraid he wants to kill me."

"And why would you think that?"

"He sent me this letter."

She passed it to me and I had a look:

Dear Harriet,

I've just been released from prison and I'm going to kill you.

Love,

Your Ex-Husband Moose

I put the letter in my jacket pocket.

"Why does he want to kill you?"

"For divorcing him."

"Maybe he just wants to reconcile."

"Read the letter again and pay closer attention."

I shrugged. Couples evolve their own language. For all I knew, "kill you" meant "let's reconcile."

"I'll pay you a hundred dollars a day to be my bodyguard," said Harriet, attempting to cross her legs and falling over backward.

"Hm. So if I work three days, I'll make five hundred dollars. I'll take the job," I said, helping her to her feet.

"You're not very good with numbers, are you?"

"I'll stick with you twenty-four/nine, and if this Moose character shows up—why is he called Moose? Does he have big ears shaped like antlers?"

"He's a very large man."

"Does he ever lock his enormous ears in combat with rival males?"

"You were saying, if Moose shows up?"

"If he shows up, I'll give him a hug he'll never forget."

Harriet Devereaux cocked her lovely head at me.

"A hug? Is that detective slang for some sort of violence?"

"I don't use detective slang, Ms. Devereaux. Except for 'gams.' I like saying 'gams.'"

"So, you're talking about a literal hug."

"The second he shows up, I'll hug him, I promise. You have no need to worry."

"But I want protection."

"And you'll get it. I'm not afraid to use my fists. Or my arms. For hugging."

"This is crazy."

"Fists are plan C if hugging doesn't work. Hugging is both plan A and B."

"Are you some kind of pacifist?"

"You wouldn't call me a pacifist if you've ever experienced one of my firmer hugs."

I opened my arms in case she wanted a sample.

"Screw you, Organ," she said, and stormed out.

"Gams," I said, instead of goodbye.

* * *

She thought she was done with me. Little did she know, she wasn't. I was making this personal. I had a code, and my code was to make things personal. The eruption of Krakatoa. Dandruff. To me, everything was personal.

The other more important part of my code was hugging. Some guys ask for it. "I need a hug." That's how they ask for it. I hoped Moose would ask for it. Makes my job easier when they do.

But I was out of practice. I hadn't done any hugging for weeks, aside from a bartender and Mac who works the newsstand and Mac's dog.

I decided to get back up to speed with one of my regular informants, Yellow Bill. He was called Yellow Bill because "canary" is slang for an informant and canaries are yellow. He'd be called Yellow even if he didn't have jaundice, but coincidentally, he did.

"Stop hugging me," said Yellow Bill in a cowardly way (funny thing, he was also a coward).

"Is this hug okay?" I asked. "I'm out of practice."

"The hug is fine, just please let go of me."

"It's not too hard, is it?"

"What do you want?"

"I don't want to bruise you."

"Let me guess. You're looking for somebody."

"Also the duration of the hug is important."

"A man?"

"If the hug is less than six seconds you don't get the full benefit."

"Does his name start with A? B? C? . . ."

I stopped Yellow Bill when he got to M.

"Moose! You're looking for Moose," said Yellow Bill, who for some reason sounded like he was being strangled. "He's at Clancy's Bar."

"Thanks, Bill. What do I owe you?"

"Let me go, that's payment enough."

* * *

Clancy's Bar was dark, but not so dark you couldn't see the behemoth seated in the corner. He was hunched over his drink, whiskey in a garbage can he was using as a shot glass, and that other customers were using as a garbage can, throwing away their dirty cocktail napkins. Moose didn't notice because he was lost in thought. His ears were normal size; I suspected he'd had some work done.

Despite his bulk, he didn't look threatening. Could he be a giant with a heart of gold? If his heart was gold, it would be worth a lot of money, but it would have to be solid gold, which it probably wasn't or else how could he be alive? This train of thought was getting me nowhere.

It would be safest if I approached him from the side, which I did. I hugged his arm. Then I crossed over and hugged his other arm. He was oblivious.

Finally, when I was hugging his head, he said, "Can I help you?"

"My name is Derek Organ. I'm a private detective. I represent your ex-wife, Harriet."

He brightened. "Harriet?"

"That's right. Harriet Devereaux."

"She kept her maiden name. I wish she'd taken my name."

"Harriet Moose?"

He nodded as I unwrapped myself from his head and took a seat opposite him.

"I sure would like to see Harriet again," he said.

"So you can kill her?"

"No." He looked hurt. "So I can smooch her."

"Until she was dead?"

I retrieved the letter from my jacket and passed it across to Moose.

He looked it over and said, "I didn't write this."

"Harriet said you did."

"Must be some other Moose she used to be married to. I was sitting here, getting up the courage to see Harriet. I want to reconcile."

"She hired me as a bodyguard because she's afraid you'll kill her. Then she fired me when she learned I wanted to give you a hug."

"So that's what you were doing to my head."

"She hates me, and she's scared of you."

"We need to clear this up," said Moose, suddenly standing and knocking loose half a dozen ceiling tiles.

"Be honest. How was the hug?" I said as I followed him out of Clancy's.

* * *

I needed to clear up the mystery of the letter Moose said he didn't write. Moose thought we could find Harriet living in a house off Beachwood Canyon, the one they used to share. I drove there. Moose rode in the flatbed trailer I was towing. I rented it for the trip so he could stretch out and be comfortable, maybe take a nap.

As I drove and Moose slept, it occurred to me that when Moose said he didn't write the letter, he might have been lying. Here I was, driving him straight to Harriet, making it convenient for him to kill her, and if that were the case, I hoped he'd thank me.

"We're here," said Moose groggily. I parked in front of a cute bungalow, and we walked to the front door.

"You think she changed the locks?" I said.

Moose tore the front door off its hinges. "Honey, I'm home," he bellowed.

I followed him into the front room.

Harriet was sitting in an easy chair. "Well," she said, "if it isn't my ex-husband and the Hugging Detective."

She was calm. If a massive man I thought was going to kill me had just torn off my front door, I think I'd be more concerned.

"Hello, babe," said Moose.

"Good job, Organ," said Harriet. "You brought a killer into my living room."

"In all fairness, he entered first."

"You're a crappy bodyguard," she sneered.

"I hugged his head," I said in my own defense.

Moose tried slouching a little to make himself look smaller, but he only looked sadder.

"Babe, I'd never do anything to hurt you. I love you. I want to reconcile with you. What possible reason would I have to kill you?"

"If I could think of a good reason," she said, "don't you think I would've put it in the letter?"

"Huh?" said Moose. "*You* wrote it?"

"Of course I wrote it."

"Hoo boy," I said. "This is awkward. Group hug?"

"No group hug, Organ. But thanks for bringing Moose here." Harriet reached into the cushions of her chair, pulled out a .32 revolver, and emptied six slugs into the big man. He died on the spot, but since there was no room for him to topple over, he remained standing.

"He was always crowding me," she said.

I shrugged. "He crowded everybody. He couldn't help it."

"I needed my freedom. It would never have worked between us."

"Well, it certainly won't work now."

"There won't be any witnesses," she said, reloading her gun.

I glanced around the room, looking for witnesses. Maybe someone was hiding in the credenza.

Unless . . .

Uh-oh. I had to think fast.

If I ran straight at her, she'd shoot me before I could hug her. I could try for a side hug, but again, she'd see me coming.

As I was weighing my options, I leaned on Moose's upright corpse. He toppled over and fell on Harriet, pinning her to the floor.

It was a simple matter to pry the gun out of Harriet's fingers.

Then I hugged her hand.

* * *

I left it up to Detective Frank Krane and his boys from Homicide to drag Harriet out from under Moose's corpse, put the cuffs on her, and take her away.

When I tried to hug Detective Krane, he knocked me to the floor. Then he and his team took turns kicking me, making it difficult to hug their fast-moving feet.

They took me down to the station, where Krane and I discussed the case as he continued to kick me.

"What's with all the hugging, Organ? Are you a pacifist?"

"That's funny. The lady asked me the same thing a while ago. *Oof.*"

"You can't go around hugging all the time. It makes people nervous. Why don't you carry a gun like the other private detectives?"

"Getting a gun license is a hassle. Much harder than getting a hugging license."

I reached into my wallet and showed Krane my hugging license.

"Hm," said Krane. "Okay, Organ. You're free to go. But keep your arms to yourself."

That hugging license had gotten me out of a jam and was worth every penny I'd paid for it down at city hall. It cost twelve dollars. I'd given them a twenty and gotten two dollars back.

I think that's right.

PLEASE, NO MORE NATIONAL ANYTHING DAYS

Life, liberty, and the pursuit of isolation. That's what it says in my personal Declaration of Independence, and that's all you need to know about me, unless it's *life, liberty, and keeping people at arm's distance*, in my other personal Declaration of Independence.

Look, I'm fine being around people. If I wasn't I wouldn't have a job, would I? I sit in my cubicle every day and do my work, thankful that people stay on the other side of the electrified fence that surrounds me. (The fence is imaginary.) I'm happy to say I give off a stay-on-the-other-side-of-my-imaginary-electrified-fence vibe.

I hate social media, as you can imagine, because it's social. Nevertheless, I permit myself a quick look at Facebook once in a while, hoping to see a cat video. (I don't like cats, just cat videos.)

The posts on social media that make me crazy are the "National *Anything* Days" and the people who honor them. "In honor of National Toffee Day, I'm eating toffee!" "In honor of National Siblings Day, I'm eating my siblings!" I wish it said that. It actually *does* say that in my imaginary Facebook account.

Who makes up these national days? Who decides what they will be? I told myself I wouldn't think about it anymore. I lied.

* * *

I was doing pretty good not thinking about it, letting National Flapjack Day and National Colorful Socks Day pass without incident.

But one day a real post caught my attention:

I'm celebrating National Be Nice to Quentin Major Day by being nice to Quentin Major!

My name is Quentin Major; you can imagine my surprise.

"I brought you a cup of coffee. Milk and two sugars, that's how you like it, isn't it?" said a young lady on the other side of my make-believe fence.

"Why . . . yes," I said, imagining a hole she could pass the coffee through. Which she did.

"I'm Marcy," she said.

"I'm . . . Quentin Major." I was shocked and could barely utter my own name.

"I know. Your picture's on Facebook. Happy National Be Nice to Quentin Major Day, Quentin."

I nodded stupidly.

"If you need anything at all, just ask. Again, my name is Marcy."

She walked away.

What was going on? I didn't have time to research why I was the subject of a national day. I was too busy imagining holes so people could pass me coffee, doughnuts, and cash. Which they did.

I must confess, I enjoyed the jealous look on the face of my coworker in the next cubicle, Odious Gene Pratt. It's hard to imagine Odious Gene having a more odious looking face than his usual resting face, but he did, odious plus jealous, because of the attention I was getting.

With all the coffee I was drinking I had to make frequent trips to the bathroom, passing through a gauntlet of compliments.

"You're looking really handsome today, Quentin."

"Beautiful hair, Quentin."

"Nice butt, Quentin."

"Take as much time as you need in the bathroom. We look forward to cleaning it later."

And so forth, all day long. I let my guard down. I removed the fence altogether, as well as the moat and crocodiles.

And then, just like that, I was back home, and the day was done.

What had just happened? And why? I lie in bed with a sense of relief, knowing tomorrow the office would return to normal. People would no longer be nice to me just because it was my special day. I imagined topping off my fence with razor wire.

I fell asleep and had a nightmare. I dreamed that every day was National Be Nice to Quentin Major Day.

I woke up in a non-imaginary cold sweat.

* * *

"Good morning, Quentin. This is for you."

Marcy again. She offered me a homemade apple pie.

"No, no. Be Nice to Quentin Day is over."

"I know. Today is National Bake an Apple Pie for Quentin Major Day."

"Ah. I didn't check. So today suggests being nice to me in a specific way."

"Yes."

For an instant I felt disappointment. Then I shrugged it off. Hey, I liked apple pie.

"Pass me the pie. Careful of the razor wire. Um . . . thank you, Marcy."

She nodded, smiled, and took her leave, her duty discharged.

Did I say I liked apple pie? I thought I did, until there were so many pies in my cubicle and on the floor surrounding my chair that the apple stench made me gag.

And it didn't stop at the office. People kept sailing apple pies into the back of the U-Haul pie trailer I rented to get my pastries home.

It was worse with the mittens.

"Here you go," said Marcy, on National Knit a Pair of Mittens for Quentin Major Day.

Marcy couldn't knit. One of the mittens barely fit over my thumb. The other mitten was the size of a sleeping bag.

"Thank you, Marcy."

Marcy managed half a smile and hurried away, embarrassed about her lousy knitting job.

In fact, all the mittens I got were lousy. Knitted from burlap, steel wool, fiberglass, linguine. Still, I felt obliged to bring them all home in the U-Haul.

National Take Quentin Major to the Zoo Day was another disaster. I was surrounded by people ushering me to each cage and habitat. I couldn't see any animals through the crowd.

"I'm finished!" I shouted, elbowing my way to the exit. I went home. I burned the mittens. I ate as many apple pies as I could before I puked, then I put the rest out on the curb.

* * *

The fence was back up, this time a real electrified fence. It kept Marcy and everyone else at bay on National Wrap Quentin Major in Tar Paper Day, National Make a Plaster Cast of Quentin Major's Head Day, and National Tickle Quentin Major Really Hard Until He Screams Day.

* * *

The new fence worked. My coworkers were terrified of being electrocuted. Everything was back to normal—until one day, when I observed Marcy walk right past me—ignoring me—so she could bring coffee to Odious Gene Pratt!

I checked Facebook. Was it National Be Nice to Odious Gene Pratt Day? No! It was National Leaf Blower Day. Nothing to do with Odious Gene Pratt. Marcy was being nice on her own dime, oblivious to his odiousness.

I needed to get her back. I needed her to be nice to me again. I needed more national days.

* * *

I decided to go straight to the top, to the Department of National Days in Washington, DC, in an area of our nation's capital only accessible by walking through a vast field of poppies, getting drowsy, falling asleep, and then waking up when it snowed on you.

When I finally got to the National Days building, and after getting some lip from a guard in a silly green coat, I entered. I shoved a lion and a straw man aside and entered the chamber of the big man himself: the Great and Powerful National Day Decider.

"I need more national days named after me," I said to the oversize head floating in smoke and flame.

"Sorry," intoned the decider. "You've already had your share of National Days."

I'd traveled a long way and wasn't taking no for an answer.

My little dog—I forgot to mention, I had a little dog with me. It was one of those impulse buys, where afterward you think, *Why did I buy a dog?* I don't even like dog videos, but here I was stuck with a real one. I hadn't named him yet but was thinking of calling him Momo or something. Anyway, my little yapper pulled a curtain aside with his teeth, revealing an ordinary man on the other side, operating the controls of the oversize head. The man was dressed the way I imagined marketing consultants dressed.

"Ha! You're nothing but a marketing consultant," I ventured.

"So what if I am?"

Bingo. "Give me more special days so Marcy will be nice to me."

"No. Your days were failures."

"They weren't failures. I enjoyed it when Marcy was nice to me, mostly."

"You don't get it, do you, Quentin? It was never about you."

"If not me, then who was it about?"

"Everyone you came in contact with. I'd been hired to sell more coffee, more pie crust, more tar paper, more linguine for mittens. But the numbers weren't there. So you're history. It's time for a new plan."

"No!" I flew into a rage, and so did my little dog, Jojo, who bit the consultant on the shin and peed all over his big-head control booth.

I dashed out of the chamber, climbed a staircase, and stood on a tall platform.

"Listen, everyone!" I called to all the workers at the Department of National Days below who were all wearing green. "The only reason for national days is to sell people more stuff!"

The crowd nodded. I guess they already knew.

I told them about my dog peeing in the decider's chamber, and they seemed to get a kick out of that.

As I left the building, I left little Bobo behind, certain he'd be in good hands.

* * *

I got what I wanted, just not in the way I expected.

One day before I went to work, I had the foresight to check Facebook, where someone posted:

I'm so excited! It's National Throw Something Heavy at Quentin Major Day!

Clearly the decider was angry, probably because of Coco biting him.

I called in sick.

Later I needed groceries. But as I stepped out the door of my apartment building, out of nowhere came a hail of sandbags, cinder blocks, anvils, bowling balls, and baby grand pianos.

I'll call for a delivery, I thought, and went back inside.

I stayed home the next day too, on National Break Quentin Major's Fingers Day.

Was this to be my life now? Trapped in my apartment as a series of increasingly violent National Quentin Major Days unfolded.

For a short time, it seemed the storm was over. National Pitted Olive Day. National Dog Collar Day. National Furniture Casters for Hardwood Floors Day. The days passed without incident.

I finally felt bold enough to leave my apartment building.

Big mistake. I should have checked Facebook.

On the sidewalk was an idling pickup truck. Marcy sat behind the wheel.

"It's National Drive Over Quentin Major's Foot Day," she exclaimed cheerfully.

I turned to reenter my apartment building, then hesitated.

What was wrong with me? After a lifetime of isolation, could I be suddenly overwhelmed by a longing for social interaction, no matter how painful? Was I so starved for attention that I would permit a young woman to drive over my foot in a Toyota Tacoma?

Later at home, I relaxed with my foot up, thinking:

I bet Odious Gene Pratt wishes he had an orthopedic boot like mine.

I'D LIKE TO THANK ALL THE SICK PEOPLE

The young man looked at me like I was crazy. "What?!" he said. "No! Of course I didn't bring a scalpel!"

I see this attitude a lot. It's as if some people come to my clinic to not be operated on.

My name is Dr. Adam Cutter, and I'm a surgeon. Isn't that funny? I suppose with a name like Cutter I had to become a surgeon, the same way Steve Wynn had to build casinos. Wynn, Win, right? And even though Christopher Plummer was a fine actor, he might've been an even better plumber. Something to think about.

I know I'm rambling, but rambling is part of my bedside manner. If I ramble in a friendly way it takes the patient's mind off their upcoming surgery. I feel it's important to practice my bedside manner, one of many skills a doctor needs if he hopes to win the award for Best Doctor.

My bedside manner was really getting put to the test with my current patient, a nervous young man probably suffering from a ruptured appendix. I wouldn't know for sure until I opened him up, and I couldn't do that until he provided me with a scalpel.

"What was your name again, pal?" I asked.

"Oww . . . Alan . . . oww . . . ," he said, his hand on his lower abdomen.

"Well, Alan, if you'd thought ahead and brought surgical instruments, we could be well into the procedure by now."

"Instruments are provided by the—oww—hospital!"

"This isn't a hospital, it's the Cutter Clinic."

I mean, really. Was it my fault he made the choice to come to my clinic to save a few bucks? We're cheap because we cut back on "frills," like forceps and beds. And when I say "we," I mean "me," because nurses are also "frills."

"But why?" said Alan with pleading eyes.

"The Cutter Clinic was founded on a philosophy, and you can read about it here," I said, handing him a brochure.

"Oww!"

"Okay, I'll read it to you. 'Helping patients help themselves.' That's it in a nutshell. One thing the academy looks for when they select Best Doctor is a concise philosophy of healing."

Alan, now on his knees, seemed more interested in his own pain than in my philosophy of healing. No matter. It was a sound philosophy, far more sound than that of my arch rival.

His name is Dr. Sidney Hacker. (For every Barbara Boxer who's not a boxer, there's a Sidney Hacker who's a surgeon.) We physicians form a tightly knit community, except for me and Sidney Hacker, who I'd love to see crushed under a falling cinder block.

Hacker's philosophy of healing is to keep his patients conscious during surgery, distracting them by showing a Wile E. Coyote versus Road Runner cartoon. It sounds good in theory, but it's not practical for surgeries longer than six minutes. I suggested he show a feature-length animated film, but he called that a stupid suggestion, and that's why I hope spiders lay eggs in his skull.

In spite of Hacker being a jerk who should bleed through his eyes, he's been getting good press and is this year's favorite to win Best Doctor. I desperately needed to catch up.

"Get me scalpels, forceps, clamps, and a Langenbeck retractor. It's similar to a regular retractor except it says 'Langenbeck' on the side," I said to Alan, now writhing on the floor.

"L-A-N-..." Alan trembled as he tried to write the shopping list on the back of the brochure.

"Let me do that," I said, taking the list. "And pick up some anesthetic. If all you can find is booze, get Jack Daniel's. Off you go."

He stumbled out the door.

While I waited for his return I fantasized about joining the esteemed ranks of previous Best Doctors: Dr. Hans Mangler, Dr. Marvin Amputator, Dr. Sylvia Sawbones.

Before long a shaky Alan returned with a shopping bag full of surgical instruments, two-fifths of Jack Daniel's, and three police officers.

"We found this guy lying on the sidewalk," said the sergeant in charge. "He had a brochure with your address on it."

"Thanks very much. Want to stick around for the operation?"

The sergeant and his men brightened. I guess they'd never been asked before. Grinning from ear to ear, they followed me and Alan into the OR.

Alan stretched out on the table. The officers and I gathered around him and shared the Jack. Then I got down to business. It was fun to have a police sergeant next to me giving me a scalpel when I'd say "Scalpel," like a doctor on a TV doctor show. Then he'd say, "Freeze!" like a cop on a TV cop show.

The operation was a success. But the event turned sour when the sergeant got a call.

"What?" he said. "Yeah, they're both here."

The sergeant put away his phone.

"You're under arrest," he said to me.

"Are you still pretending you're on a TV show?" I said.

"'Fraid not," said the sergeant. He pointed at Alan. "He walked out of the surgical supply store without paying. You're both under arrest for shoplifting."

Alan had stolen the instruments. And I had written the shopping list, making me an accessory.

* * *

Prison wasn't bad. I was popular there, way more popular than the regular prison doctor who used his own instruments. The prisoners wanted to be challenged. They enjoyed making scalpels, having had experience fashioning shivs out of toothbrushes and razor blades. One enterprising inmate made forceps from an old Bible.

I was so well liked they named me Best Prison Doctor, not a real award, just a nice gesture.

The one drawback to being in the joint was that I lost ground to Sidney Hacker, now scoring points by performing surgery to full-length Disney animated musicals. Was he giving me credit for the idea? Pardon me while I snort laugh. Snort. Ha.

Vegas oddsmakers placed me a distant second. When I was released I had to get busy.

My plan was to visit Dr. Hacker in disguise and say I was sick. I arrived at his clinic wearing a bushy wig, a fake beard, and a fat suit. I chose this costume because I figured while he was cutting through the thick fat suit I'd have plenty of time to discredit him.

On the way into his clinic, I passed a daughter helping her mother out the front door.

"Are you here to see Dr. Hacker?" the mother said. "Oh, he's wonderful!"

"Really?" I mumbled through my fake beard.

"He removed my gall bladder during the 'Be Our Guest' number from *Beauty and the Beast*. I didn't feel a thing."

She showed me her Blu-ray. "Would you like to borrow it?"

"He made you bring your own movie?!" That's another idea he stole from me. "Thanks, but no. I have *The Little Mermaid*." I lied.

I sat in Dr. Hacker's waiting room, thinking if I died on his table it would really discredit his philosophy of healing, wondering how I could pull that off.

Before I could work out the details, Dr. Hacker entered the waiting room.

"What seems to be the trouble?"

There he was, Sidney Hacker, standing there with his bushy hair, beard, and fat belly. It was then I realized I had subconsciously disguised myself as the most disgusting human being I could think of.

"I need a carotid endarectomy," I said, making something up. "And don't bother sterilizing your scalpel. I brought my own!"

I produced the scalpel I'd gotten from Alan months ago and waved it in the air.

"Cutter!" he said. "I knew it was you. At first I thought I was looking in the mirror. But then I realized your fat suit is newer and cleaner than mine."

"And my beard is longer and my hair is bushier. Everything about me is better than you, Hacker. You'll never win the award."

"Says you!"

We shed our fat suits and went at it, struggling in Hacker's waiting room, tumbling over magazine racks, slipping on year-old People magazines.

"Ha!" said Hacker, producing his own scalpel.

We dueled with scalpels. We tried to perform swashbuckling moves but only succeeded in grazing each other's knuckles.

"Ow!"

"Ow!"

"Wait! Look there!" Hacker said, pointing to a security camera high up in the corner. "The Academy of Doctors installed that camera."

"Why?"

"So they could observe my philosophy of healing in action."

"And what does having a scalpel fight have to do with your philosophy?"

"Nothing."

"It has nothing to do with mine either."

We'd blown it. We sat in the waiting room, licking our bleeding knuckles.

"Well, hell," I said. "Now neither of us will win Best Doctor."

"Nope."

After a moment I said, "We'd better bandage our knuckles."

"Yep. Hey, we could bandage each other while watching *Aladdin*. Ever seen it?"

"Are you kidding? '*A whole new world . . .*'"

* * *

That year the award for Best Doctor was given to Dr. Roland Mutilator, whose philosophy of healing was to operate on patients while they rode theme park roller coasters. His survival rate was low, but the academy didn't care, because these days flashy surgeons get all the attention. Dr. Hacker and I had had enough.

We merged our clinics. Now that the pressure to compete was off, we went back to the basics: surgery performed by surgeons with their own instruments, under anesthesia, without cartoons.

And together we created a new philosophy of healing, which was: to heal.

And drink Jack Daniel's. After the surgery.

DRUM BUTTONS

Dierdre Downey scanned the faces of the six men seated around the conference room table, each one licking his lips with anticipation.

Hayes Sr., silver-haired founder of the company, said, "Ms. Downey, please don't keep us in suspense. What were the results of your focus group study?"

Dierdre smiled a cool half-smile and nodded.

"Drum buttons."

There was a pause of not more three minutes. Then Hayes Jr., a carbon copy of his father, spoke up.

"Sorry. Drum—?"

"Drum buttons," said Dierdre, with another nod and half-smile.

All eyes turned to Hayes Sr. *How do we react?*

"Ah," said Hayes Sr. "Well."

"That may require clarification," ventured Quinn, a young up-and-comer.

"Of course." Dierdre reached into her oversized leather satchel, produced six spiral-bound reports with DRUM BUTTONS embossed the covers, and distributed them to the executives. Each man opened his report to find a single off-white sheet of paper with the words *drum buttons* centered on the page.

"Well," said Cutler, another young executive, "that answers a lot of questions, doesn't it, Mr. Hayes?"

"No."

"When I say 'a lot,' I mean 'next to none.'"

"Ms. Downey, forgive me for being dense . . ."

"You're forgiven, Mr. Hayes," she said, working her cool half-smile.

"What exactly does *drum buttons* have to do with launching a new toothpaste?"

"You expect me to do your work for you?" said Dierdre, changing her half-smile to a disapproving pout.

"No, no, no," said every man in the room.

"I suppose you also want me to get your coffee."

"We're all good on coffee," said Hayes Jr.

"Actually, I could use another cup," said Cutler.

"You're fired!" shouted Hayes Sr., and Cutler scurried out of the room.

"Gentlemen," said Dierdre, "I supervise focus groups. That's all I do."

"Of course."

"Obviously," said Dierdre, indicating the report, "this doesn't apply to every demographic."

The executives breathed a sigh of relief.

I'm lying, she thought. *It applies to every demographic. Every test result was the same.*

"And so, gentlemen," she said, rising, "I will leave you to make the best use of these findings."

The executives stood.

"Thank you, Ms. Downey," said Hayes Sr.

Dierdre smiled. "It's been a pleasure, Mr. Hayes." *Also lying.*

When Dierdre was gone, the executives reread the report. Some made notes in the margins.

"I tell you, Dad," said Hayes Jr., "I'm befuddled."

"We're all befuddled. That doesn't mean we shouldn't use this study to full advantage. The American consumer has spoken. We ignore his or her input at our peril."

Eventually, Quinn spoke up. "If I may, Mr. Hayes, I believe the phrase *drum buttons* refers to buttons shaped like tiny drums."

Hayes Sr. narrowed his eyes.

"I'm sorry I said that. I'll fire myself," said Quinn, leaving the room.

* * *

In an empty corner of the parking structure, Dierdre took up smoking. After finding a discarded cigarette and lighter, and watching a YouTube instructional video, she was soon puffing away, choking and feeling calmer.

You pulled if off, girl. I'm proud of you, she said to herself.

Thank you, she replied to herself.

You had the guts to face the client armed with only two words. And not just any two words, but two nonsensical words, she said.

I know. I was there too, she replied.

Drum buttons.

Focus groups don't lie. That's what Dierdre believed in every fiber of her Pilates-sculpted body. That's why she'd built Downey Research Services into the most trusted focus group company in America.

Drum buttons.

She no longer ran group sessions. She had facilitators to run the sessions for her, and now she just popped her head into the meetings. To Dierdre, the apex of success was popping her head into meetings.

Last Tuesday, she had popped her head into a meeting of six women ages 30 to 45, run by one of her favorite young facilitators, Justin, who had laid his head on the conference table and was weeping.

Dierdre rushed into the room, put her arm around Justin, and hurried him out the door.

In the hallway, Justin blubbered, "I asked, 'Do you prefer tea or coffee in the morning?' They said, 'Drum buttons.' I asked, 'If tea, do you take it with sweetener?' They said, 'Drum buttons.' 'Would you ever try presweetened tea?'—"

"Those bitches are being paid. I won't let them get away with this," said Dierdre. Leaving Justin blubbering in the hallway, she stormed back into the boardroom and faced the women with her arms folded.

"It's not funny, you know? Giving the same nonsense answer to every question."

A large black woman named Lola, who seemed to be the leader, rose to her feet, towering over Dierdre.

"Ma'am, we answered your questions independently, unaware of what the others were writing."

"Drum buttons?"

"That's honestly how I felt."

"That's how I felt too," said a woman seated next to the leader.

"Me too."

All six asserted that "drum buttons" best expressed their feelings concerning presweetened breakfast tea.

"But . . . but what does that even mean?!" said Dierdre.

Lola shrugged. "You want us to do your work for you?"

In every room of the Downey Research Services building, the story was the same. No matter the demographic—teens, preschoolers, seniors, active members of the military. No matter the focus group subject—mouthwash, cookies, beer, weighted blankets, romantic comedies, hemorrhoid creams. Every potential consumer expressed the same response, whether verbal or written.

"Did anyone from any of your groups have a response that *wasn't* 'drum buttons'?" Dierdre asked of the dozen facilitators now gathered in her office.

Miguel, the youngest, eager to make a name for himself, said, "Yes! I had an eighty-two-year-old man say, 'Stop!' to me."

"Stop what?"

Miguel hung his head. "Stop slapping him after he kept saying 'drum buttons.'"

"I don't think this is a conspiracy," mused Dierdre. "I've never believed those conspiracy theories about secret consumer groups. So if we're sure these results were arrived at independently, . . ."

Everyone nodded.

"Then, in order to preserve the integrity of my company, I have no choice but to present 'drum buttons' to our clients."

Back in the parking structure, Dierdre drew deeply on her cigarette. This was called a drag, she had learned. She dropped the cigarette on the ground and crushed it out with her shoe, as if she'd been doing it all her life.

Three more meetings today, she thought. *Hope I find another pack of cigarettes.*

* * *

"Remember when people were told they could be movie stars if their teeth were whiter?" mused Hayes Sr., chuckling.

"That was before my time, Dad," said Hayes Jr.

"It was before my time too!" bellowed Hayes Sr. "You're fired!"

As Hayes Jr. trudged out of the screening room, the lights dimmed. The executives turned their attention to the screen.

"Having whiter doesn't guarantee you can become a movie star," said the handsome young man with the dazzling smile seated across from his beautiful date during their candlelit dinner.

"I don't want to be a movie star," she said, shooting him a dazzling smile in return. "At least, not until after dinner."

The blinding beams of light reflected off the couple's teeth form letters on the screen:

DRUM BUTTON TOOTHPASTE

The letters morph into:

BE A MOVIE STAR

* * *

"I'm a working mom," says a working mom to the camera. "I don't always have time to cook for my family. Thank goodness for Drum Buttons."

Three children at the table eat from bowls filled with pasta shaped something like tiny drums in a red sauce. They turn to the camera.

"Yay, Drum Buttons! They're dope!"

* * *

"If you recall, General," said the mysterious man with the eyepatch, "you disbanded our elite group four years ago. You said it was unethical, turning soldiers into mindless fighting machines."

"I recall that vividly, Patchy."

"I have bad news. One of our men never got the message. He's pissed off. And he's coming for you."

The general's cigar dropped out of his mouth and onto his desk.

"So what can I do?"

"There's nothing you can do. He's unstoppable. He's a Drum Button."

Don't miss Liam Neeson in:

THE DRUM BUTTON PROTOCOL

* * *

Dierdre sat behind the wheel of her Drum Button DB-5, waiting for her next meeting. She lit up another cigarette, now an old hand at smoking, no longer needing the instructional video. She was up to two packs of Drum Button Ultra-Lites a day.

She laughed a laugh bordering on hysteria. She could do no wrong. Why were the results of a hundred focus groups the same? Was it because people saw nothing but Drum Buttons wherever they looked, and so began to think that's what they wanted? Was it a crazy loop? Brainwashing or some shit?

It didn't matter.

* * *

"Drum buttons," said Dierdre. She passed out recycled reports from a cough syrup group, secure in the knowledge that these people, whoever the hell they were, wouldn't know the difference.

The group studied the report. A kernel of unease formed in Dierdre's stomach and began to grow. Somehow these people were different. Cooler, more calculating. Scarier. It made Dierdre long for the company of the nice toothpaste guys.

Scariest of all was the man who wasn't there. His face appeared on a video screen, his teeth gleaming with Drum Button brightness, his hair held in place with Drum Button spray volumizer.

The video man, whose name was Sebastian Omnisphere, said to the group, "I don't have the report in front of me. What does it say? What am I supposed to stand for? Is it Drum Buttons? I bet it's Drum Buttons. I hope it's Drum Buttons. I've already made notes on a speech in support of Drum Buttons."

Dierdre thought, *Time for a smoke.* "Gentlemen, it's been a pleasure." She rose from her chair.

"Sit down," said a rumpled older man, a veteran of the political scene. He ran his fingers through his stringy hair.

"Sebastian?"

"Yes, Mel?"

"We have a problem."

Mel threw his report violently across the table. Then he realized he had timed his gesture poorly. For a moment he felt old, then he picked up the report.

"This report is useless!" he said, throwing the report, this time with improved timing.

"What do you mean, Mel?" said Sebastian.

"I mean," said Mel, turning his gaze on Dierdre, "this is someone else's study!"

Suddenly she had no energy for denial. "Okay. This is the result of a cough syrup group. But so what? The result will always be 'drum buttons.'"

"No," said Mel. He reached under his chair and produced a different report in a different colored binder. Opening the binder to the first page, he read:

"Red axle biscuits."

"What?!"

"Red axle biscuits."

"Oh, come on. Somebody's just stringing words together."

"No, Ms. Downey. These are the results of a reputable group."

"Conducted by who?"

"By us," said a dozen voices in unison. From behind a screen stepped Justin, Miguel, and ten other of Dierdre's former employees. She noted with horror they were wearing track suits with a Red Axle Biscuit logo.

"Traitors," Dierdre mumbled under her breath.

"No, Ms. Downey," said Miguel. "You're the traitor. A traitor to the American consumer."

"That's right," said Justin, no longer weeping, now in control. "You thought you could con these people with old results. Where's your big talk about integrity now?"

"We respect the consumer," said Miguel. "We listen. We respond."

"So apparently my Drum Button notes are useless. What do I say?" said Sebastian Omnisphere on the video screen. "I promise to stop the flood of illegal Red Axle Biscuits into this country. Or maybe the Constitution guarantees the right of every American to bear a Red Axle Biscuit—"

"Shut up. *We'll* write the speeches," groaned Mel.

* * *

On a chilly October day. Dierdre shivered on a park bench and drew her threadbare Drum Button overcoat around her, wishing she still had a job so she could afford a fleece-lined Red Axle Biscuit parka. Everyone had one.

I'm done with it. I'm done with this whole foul, brainwashed culture. Maybe I'll move to Costa Rica and raise bananas, she thought, as she lit another Red Axle Biscuit Gold 100 from the one she'd just smoked down to the filter.

I'll Google Costa Rica tonight. In the meantime, maybe a movie. I've heard good things about RED AXLE BISCUIT IV: RISE OF THE BISCUITS . . .

THE PIÑATA REPAIRMAN

My hero, steel magnate Andrew Carnegie said, "The first man gets the oyster, the second man gets the shell." I'm not sure what he meant, but it probably had something to do with metaphoric oysters and literal steel.

I've tried to follow his example. In my case it's not literal steel, but literal busted-up piñatas restored to their former glory. I'm Ben Sharply, the Piñata Repairman, and it's my dream to build an empire like Mr. Carnegie, and then endow Sharply Hall and Sharply Mellon University.

I didn't always have this sense of purpose. Twenty years ago I was a young repairman, learning how to repair everything all the other repairmen were repairing—refrigerators, air conditioners, screen doors. Until I had an epiphany. Why waste time? Why not specialize? Why not immerse myself in piñata repair? Did Mr. Carnegie dawdle with oil and other things that weren't steel? I think not.

Since no technical school offered classes in my chosen field, I created my own course of study. After months of observing children's birthday parties, I learned that 90 percent of piñata repair involved damage to the confectionary drum, a term that did not exist until I made it up. The confectionary drum, or drum for short, is where the goodie payload is held, prior to its release via the impact of the piñata stick, or stick. Sorry if I'm getting too technical.

When the party's over, that's when I go to work. I gather up the broken pieces of the piñata, plus the unclaimed pieces of candy, and return to my workshop. I select from over four hundred different shades of papier-mâché, a pretentious French term for wet strips of paper. For an extra fee I'll do the repair on site, in case there's another party in the same place on the same day, under the same tree branch. Still waiting for that to happen.

An average piñata job takes about four weeks. I confess, returning the piñata to the customer is the hardest part of the job, as most people never ask for my service in the first place. I'm forced to explain to them how I was the guy in overalls running around picking up piñata pieces, the guy they called the cops on. And now, I say, "Here's your paper donkey looking brand-new." Once they get over the shock and tell me how the original piñata was a T. rex, I patiently explain how I'm a donkey specialist, therefore everything I fix ends up a donkey. Then I give them the bill and they pay it, gratefully, marveling at how reasonably priced my service is, trying to force a generous gratuity on me, which I never accept.

Okay, the part about the gratuity isn't true. The only part that's true is me telling them I only do donkeys. After years of practicing my trade, I had to face the truth—most people don't want their piñatas repaired. They don't feel it's worth the expense. I would shout at them, "So what are you going to do? Throw your broken piñata into the sea where a dolphin will eat it and choke to death, thinking it's a sea donkey?"

My days were filled with frustration. I was renting an enormous, expensive warehouse for all the restored donkey piñatas nobody wanted. I couldn't afford an apartment, so I lived there. I ate Jolly Rancher candies, the green apple ones everybody hates. I slept on a donkey piñata bed, not as comfortable as it sounds.

Still I refused to give up my dream. I bet there was a time when Andrew Carnegie lived in a steel mill and slept on an ingot bed.

One night as I was drifting off to sleep, the idea hit me like a stick hitting a piñata in the confectionary drum. I would enter the marketplace and sell my work to the public. I'd call my business Ben Sharply's Like-New Pre-Owned Donkey Piñatas. Simple and elegant. I could sell them cheaply, because not only would it be the second time around for them, but they would also be filled with nasty green apple Jolly Ranchers.

From the first, business was brisk. Because they were cheap, customers bought piñatas by the dozen. I imagined they gave them to relatives, or just threw parties where everyone had their own piñata.

My grateful customers told me about the exorbitant prices other sellers charged. One guy wanted a thousand dollars for just one. Of course his piñatas were filled with hundred-dollar bills, which tells me his business model wasn't that great.

Another merchant was selling overpriced donkeys with just one piece of candy inside, a grape Jolly Rancher, the kind kids like. They'd fight over it and beat each other bloody with sticks. The guy should have been arrested, but he was bribing the law with grape candy, the kind cops like.

My prices remained low, and my business thrived. I hired a team of thirty employees whose only job was to attend parties, wait for the kid to break the piñata, then dash in and scoop up the pieces. Frequently my team outnumbered the children and had to take care not to trample the youngsters to death, which would spoil the fun for the birthday kid and the others.

I had another team who did nothing but pass me wet papier-mâché while they sang French songs. It sounds crazy but it made more sense than hiring French people.

I was on a roll. I had the feeling Andrew Carnegie was looking down on me, smiling, saying, "Look at that piñata repairman," or something even pithier involving oysters.

One morning I arose from my donkey piñata bed, now outfitted with expensive satin sheets. After breakfasting on coffee and green apple Jolly Ranchers, I went to open the front door of the store. Usually there was a line outside. Today there was a line, not of customers but of three muscular men in black suits with scarred faces and sticks (piñata sticks).

I considered keeping the door locked. Then I thought, maybe these guys are suburban parents, from one of the more violent suburbs.

I was glad I let the trio in, after learning we were all in the piñata business. They had been hired by my competitors, and we spent a few moments talking shop. I suggested we put up flyers in each other's stores. They suggested I close my business, burn my inventory, and leave town. Eyeing their sticks, I said I'd think it over.

Well, I didn't think it over long. I refused to give in. Surely Andrew Carnegie had experienced intimidation from turn-of-the-century thugs with turn-of-the-century sticks.

"Let's be reasonable," I said. "I specialize in donkeys. There are plenty of other shapes your bosses can sell."

"But donkeys are more popular than the others," said one guy, Tony "the Stick Man" Ambrose.

"Yeah, nobody likes them star-shaped ones," said Vito "Sticky" Pirelli.

"It's because the stars don't hold much candy," explained Lou "Walk Softly and Carry a Big Stick" Boca.

"I'm sorry, fellas. There's no way I'm going to fold my business."

They growled. The time had come to defend myself. Though outnumbered, I had confidence in my upper-body strength, acquired from years of molding papier-mâché. I prepared to throw the first punch.

But they were too fast for me.

In a heartbeat I was suspended from the ceiling. I watched them, upside down, as they gripped their sticks and prepared to swing. If it had been anyone but me hanging there, I might have found the scene ironically amusing.

Wishing not to end up like one of my battered donkeys, I thought fast.

"Don't forget your blindfolds," I said.

Embarrassed at the oversight, they produced blindfolds and tied them around their heads. As they felt around for their weapons I saw my chance for escape. But my bonds were too tight.

They found their weapons and began swinging. They may have been professional goons, but when it came to hitting a piñata they were rank amateurs. After five minutes of unfocused thrashing they had knocked each other out.

I dangled from the ceiling, helpless, until the papier-mâché crew arrived for work. They cut me down while singing a French song. I told them singing wasn't necessary, but they had become a tight unit.

Before the three goons woke up we took away their sticks. We gave them sour apple Jolly Ranchers and sent them on their way, as they sucked and made faces.

It was time for the violence to end. I called a meeting of the five heads of the major piñata companies. We sat down and declared a truce. To the amazement of everyone, I said I was leaving the business.

It's like this: I felt I had taken my piñata repair empire as far as it would go. I would never be as big as Andrew Carnegie. As much as I longed to be like my hero, he had steel and I had piñatas, which now seemed a limitation. I suppose I could've built a suspension bridge out of papier-mâché, but who in their right mind would ever drive over it?

No, I'll wait for another revolutionary idea to come to me. And if that doesn't work, I'll try another, and another.

How do you get to Sharply Hall? Practice!

GOD IS DRUNK. AGAIN.

And lo, God was drunk. Again.

And the owner of the Red Lion Pub didst gnash his teeth as he beheld the Lord God Almighty pissed to the eyebrows.

But the pub owner was a religious man who honored the Lord. And so he didst serve God four more shots of Jameson.

And God didst awaken in heaven at one in the afternoon the following day, unsure how he got home. And his head didst throb, and his guts didst churn, and he couldst keep nothing down, not even half a can of Diet Coke.

And God didst remember how, at the Red Lion Pub, he had ordered a Jamo and pint of San Miguel lager and listened to "Come On, Eileen" by Dexys Midnight Runners, and couldst recall nothing that followed.

And God didst return to the Red Lion later that day, on pretext of finding a lost scarf, but in truth seeking knowledge of embarrassing acts he might possibly have committed.

And the pub owner sayest, "No, we haven't found a scarf," and then recounted how God hadst sung loudly to "Tubthumping" by Chumbawamba, and attempted to make out with a twenty-two-year-old exchange student, and broke a pint glass by accident and broke eight pint glasses on purpose, and attempted to make out with a fifty-four-year-old girls' volleyball coach, and curled up on the floor weeping and cursing his life, and attempted to make out with a seventy-year-old pensioner and then attempted to make out with the old man's dog.

And hearing these things God was sore ashamed and didst swear he would go on the wagon.

And God showed great fortitude and didst not touch another drop, and attended to his celestial business, and caused the sun to rise in the east, and the tides to turn, and the rivers of the earth to flow, and a landlord in Brooklyn who had hiked the rent three times in the past year to get shingles around his waist.

But God was weary, realizing he would have to make the sun come up every morning for all eternity, and so he didst return to the Red Lion Pub, saying unto himself, "Who am I hurting?"

And once more God awakened in heaven with the shakes, and lying with him were a female flight attendant from Belgium, a Vienna string quartet, and a Guernsey cow, and the Lord couldst recall none of their names.

And God persisted in thinking he could attend to the universe, even as he found it necessary to have a shot of Jamo in his morning coffee.

But now the sun rose in the west, and the rivers flowed sideways, and God forgot to do the tides altogether.

And it came to pass that one day when God arrived at the Red Lion, there was no music, and the bottles behind the bar were chained up, and the owner and the regulars stared at God, and the owner sayest, "Take a seat."

And God, having not been born yesterday and knowing an intervention when he saw one, didst cause fire and flame to consume the Red Lion Pub and everyone in it, and following the destruction, sayest to no one in particular, "Guess I'm taking my business to the Crown and Anchor."

And lo, God's drinking didst continue at the Crown and Anchor a few blocks down the street.

And one day when God was sitting with his customary shot and beer, a denim-clad man in his fifties with shoulder-length hair and a Fu Manchu mustache placed his club soda on God's table, sat next to him, and offered his hand, saying, "How's it hangin', God? I'm Randy Baxter."

And though God avoided eye contact with him, Randy Baxter didst not take the hint and continued, "Maybe you've heard of me. I used to play lead guitar in a country rock band called Slugger Fish."

And God didst shake his head, having never heard of Randy Baxter or Slugger Fish and disliking country rock more than any other music in the cosmos.

And as God reached for his shot of Jamo, Randy Baxter grabbed God's wrist and sayeth unto him, "Listen, man, after I hit bottom, I learned the answer is never in a bottle."

And God was overcome with remorse for the sad deity he had become.

And Randy Baxter didst hug God, and God wept as Randy Baxter patted him on the back and sayest, "Come on, man, let it out."

And Randy Baxter didst put his arm around God and lead him out of the Crown & Anchor and around the corner to a Unitarian church, where nine or ten country rock musicians stood on the sidewalk, chain-smoking Camel straights.

And Randy Baxter didst escort God to the AA meeting in the basement.

And God didst say to the assembled country rock musicians, "My name is God, and I'm an alcoholic."

And the country rock musicians didst reply, "Hello, God."

And God didst follow the twelve-step program. And he didst attend daily meetings, and began smoking Camel straights, and lo, God was clean and sober for forty days and forty nights.

But ere long God's mind became troubled.

And God didst meet his sponsor, Randy Baxter, for coffee.

And Randy Baxter sayeth, "Come on, man, let it out," for he could say little else.

But God had nothing to let out, he only had questions, and he sayeth, "I have asked myself to grant myself the wisdom to accept the things I cannot change. And once I granted myself that wisdom I realized I am God and I can change everything, anytime I want. So what's the point?"

And Randy Baxter said, "Let it out, man," knowing his words sounded increasingly hollow.

And God continued, "Since I turned my will over to a higher power, which is God, which is me, does that mean I should do whatever I want me to do?"

And Randy Baxter stared at the swirls of milk in his coffee.

And God sayeth, "For instance, if I tell myself to get drunk, should I do it? After all I would be obeying the will of God, which again is me."

And Randy Baxter worried that God had just talked circles around him and would now fall off the wagon and start drinking again, and all the good work done by Randy Baxter and the sober country rock musicians would be for naught.

And Randy Baxter felt he had somehow failed God.

And God didst embrace Randy Baxter and say, "Let it out, man."

And as Randy Baxter wept, God sayeth, "I'm just messing with your mind."

And lo, God didst not fall off the wagon, not entirely, except for an occasional glass of merlot with dinner.

And God didst cause the sun to rise in the east, and the tides to turn, and the rivers of the earth to flow, and that same landlord to get shingles again, only this time in his crotch.

For lo, God was now functioning.

And out of gratitude, God didst build for Randy Baxter a great stadium.

And Randy Baxter didst form a band with his AA group, and they didst call themselves the New Slugger Fish Experience.

And they didst play a concert for the stadium packed with aging fans in vintage Slugger Fish T-shirts that were now too tight.

And they served no alcohol at the concert, only kombucha tea and chocolate chip cookies.

And the New Slugger Fish Experience didst play mostly the old stuff, slipping in a couple new tunes that didn't go over very well.

And a front-row seat and a backstage pass were reserved for God.

But God begged off, lying and saying he had stomach flu.

Because good God, country rock.

WHAT'S UP, DOC—I MEAN, EXALTED MASTER?

It's true. We only use 10 percent of our brains. I know, because there was a horrible period in my life when I used 50 percent. In addition to killing the woman I loved, I was asked to help kids with their math homework. Dark days indeed.

I am Elliott Binion, thirty-five years old, sole heir to the Binion Scented Crème Rinse fortune. You could call me a classic trust fund kid, as many people have, and after twenty years of being called a trust fund kid and getting beaten up, a change was needed, not to the trust fund part, to the getting beaten up part.

I decided to build up my body to be the perfect fighting machine. While I was busy building up my body, I hired a perfect fighting machine to do my fighting for me.

After studying hard, my repertoire of deadly martial arts included kung fu, Krav Maga, Eskrima, Bacom, and spicy duck with pineapple. I could snap a man's spine and kill him, bring him back to life, and then kill him again, thus winning many bar bets.

I'd hand strangers on the street business cards reading, "Call me a trust fund kid and see what happens."

It was great. And yet, something was missing. I had disciplined my body, but what of my mind? What about my unused 120 percent? (At that point I was using less than one percent.)

There had to be a teacher somewhere, a master of the mental arts, someone as good with his frontal lobes as I was with my fists.

* * *

J. Puckworth Zerby was an enigma, a word I plan to look up in the dictionary. He was also a trust fund kid, but a smart trust fund kid who could find Tibet on a map, so he went there.

Years later he returned, now known simply as Zerby, a man with no time for worldly pursuits or middle names.

He brought with him a female companion, shrouded in mystery and a queen-size contour sheet. Together they vanished into the Adirondack Mountains in Upstate New York, intending to pursue spiritual perfection in a spot with a strong Wi-Fi signal.

It was rumored Zerby had acquired the ability to make objects appear in the physical world, simply by thinking of them.

I was obsessed. I had to learn how to do that. The possibilities were infinite. Imagine making clean clothes appear in front of me without having to do laundry. Imagine thinking of other possibilities besides that one.

Wishing to approach Master Zerby in a state of poverty and humility, I left my Maserati in the city and took a Trailways bus upstate.

I wandered through wooded mountains, across swollen streams, over golf courses, past rustic lodges with state-of-the-art fitness centers. But no Zerby.

Lost in the foggy wooded mountains, despondent, I called Trailways and asked them to send a bus to pick me up.

Then the mountain mist cleared, and there appeared before me a magical oriental palace. Could this be the magical oriental palace I was seeking, and not some other palace?

I climbed the marble stairs to the gates. It looked like the Oriental Palace Restaurant in Chinatown, only fancier and without dead ducks in the window. The gates swung open, and I stepped forward.

At the far end of a long hallway decorated with paintings of clouds, warriors, immortal beings, and gardening tools—sat Zerby.

Gangly, imposing, he wore a silk robe adorned with beads, tassels, medals, and plastic flowers. On his head was a hat with antlers, from which dangled Christmas ornaments. I thought, *Anybody who dresses like that is asking to be slapped. His power must be formidable.*

He rose as I approached.

"Master Zerby, I am—"

"I know who you are." There was an uneasy pause.

"Tell me your name again," he said.

"Elliott Binion."

"Heir to the scented crème rinse fortune."

"The same. I wish to learn—"

"I know what you wish to learn."

Another pause. The ornaments on his antlers tinkled like wind chimes.

"Refresh my memory."

"I wish to learn to manifest objects using my mind."

"Right."

Zerby rose slowly from his chair. *Tinkle tinkle.*

"After a busy eight-hour day of working to achieve spiritual perfection, all I want to do is sit on the sofa with a frozen margarita. I have no interest in teaching," he declared. "Buzz off."

He resumed his seat. *Tinkle tinkle.*

The anger rose inside of me.

"I've spent days walking these mountains. Now I find you, and you refuse to teach me. I think you're a fraud. You won't teach me to manifest objects because you can't do it. Plus you dress like a freak."

He jumped back to his feet. *Tinkle tinkle!*

"Name a vegetable," he said.

"Okay. Cauliflow—"

"Carrot it is! Watch!"

Zerby wrinkled his brow, then held his arms out, palms facing down.

"Move to your right a little bit."

I moved, and it was a good thing I did, because beams of shimmering energy shot out of Zerby's hands, focusing on the spot on the floor where I had been standing, focusing as one might use a magnifying glass to converge the sun's rays and burn a hole in a newspaper or a friend's forearm.

Zerby closed his hands into fists, shutting off the energy beams.

And there on the floor—where no carrot had been before—was a carrot!

Zerby fell back into his chair, exhausted from the effort. *Tinkle.*

"It's a trick," I said.

"It's not a trick," said Zerby, and to prove his point, produced another carrot in his right hand and poked me in the eye with it.

"Ow. Okay, I want to learn to do that."

"It's easy. You grab it by the thick end and thrust—"

"I mean, I want to materialize things with my mind."

"Were you listening when I said I have no interest in teaching?"

Tinkle tinkle tinkle . . .

A higher-pitched tinkle approached from behind. I turned.

She moved as if her feet didn't touch the ground. She was young, exotic, perfect. She wore tiny bells in her raven hair. Her almond eyes held the promise of Asian sensuality. Her porcelain hands held a book titled *The Promise of Asian Sensuality.*

"I am Kim," she said, bowing her head.

"I am Elliott," I said, using my hand to hide my swollen eye.

"Zerby, you must take on Elliott as a student."

"You know I don't want any students."

"I'm going crazy with boredom!" She stamped her foot. "While you pursue spiritual perfection, I could use some company." She turned to me. "I achieved spiritual perfection two weeks ago," she explained, opening her kimono to reveal the corresponding merit badge.

Zerby sighed, aware he'd lose the argument.

"If you don't take on Elliott as a student, I will pout the Pout of a Thousand Maidens."

Zerby shuddered. "Very well."

Kim shot me a look of spiritual perfection, and I felt the need for a cold shower.

Thus began my rigorous training with mind master Zerby, far more demanding than martial arts, in my quest to manifest objects on the physical plane.

For hours I sat outside, naked in the snow, meditating, picturing the object I desired to manifest, any object at all, Zerby said, as he traced the shape of a carrot in the air with his finger.

I was obsessed, and so after my day outdoors, I would bring a wheelbarrow of slush to my austere cubicle and sit in it for another thirty minutes until it melted. Finally, exhausted, I'd retire to the kitchen and sleep in the deep freeze.

Nothing disturbed my focus, not even the mental picture of me and Kim in a sauna playing backgammon.

Somehow I summoned the grit that had enabled me to rise from my humble beginnings as a privileged trust fund kid.

And it happened.

Early one morning, as I sat in meditation, my body began to vibrate, starting at the base of my spine and climbing to the crown of my head. Before I knew it I was shaking like a Brookstone massage chair. I heard a freight train in my ears, impossible, I thought, since the nearest tracks were twenty feet away. A ray of light painfully burst from the center of my forehead, and I hoped the hole in my head would heal before ants could crawl in.

The light blasted a patch in the snow in front of me. When the smoke cleared and my vision returned, I saw it:

An orange.

In the space where there was previously no orange, there was an orange.

"Master Zerby!" I shouted.

He came at once, running out of the palace to the spot where I sat in meditation, stopping when he saw what I was pointing to. He sighed heavily. "Not very big, is it?"

"It's a mandarin orange. They're very sweet."

"Mm-hm. Well," he said philosophically, "at least you got the color right."

And with that he wandered back to the palace.

I was stunned. I felt like a success and a failure simultaneously, with the successful feeling lasting ten minutes and the failure feeling lingering for days.

I kept trying. A week passed. Then the same vibration, the same laser blast from my forehead . . .

A honeydew melon.

"Master Zerby!"

He stepped out of the palace, glanced at the melon which was large and could be seen from the porch, then made a U-turn.

I thought the melon was an improvement. I thought I was on the right track, but Zerby's dismissive behavior was crushing my spirit.

I sat with Kim in my cubicle, eating a cucumber tomato avocado salad, the ingredients of which I had reified with my mind, except for the lemon dressing, which Kim found in the pantry.

"Don't be depressed," she said, touching my strong manly hand with her hand, smaller but no less attractive. "Zerby's narrow-minded. If you're not manifesting carrots he couldn't care less."

"How can you stay with someone like that?"

"It was fun at first. Zerby was always full of sparkling witticisms. And if the conversation lagged, he would make a carrot appear under my bottom, causing me to leap to my feet, startled. It was hilarious."

"But even a good joke gets stale. Why haven't you learned to make things with your mind?"

"I don't like sitting in the snow bare-assed. How old do you think I am, Elliott?"

"I would guess, five hundred years."

"I'm twenty-two."

"Sorry, I thought you were some sort of ancient . . . Please continue."

Kim's suddenly wrapped her arms around me and squeezed. I inhaled deeply the scent of her Asian sensuality and the lemon dressing she'd spilled on her kimono.

"I can't go anywhere. I'm virtually a prisoner. I'm wasting my life with a carrot-obsessed martinet. If I stay another day I'll go mad. Please take me away."

I reluctantly pried Kim's arms from around my neck.

"I'd love to take you away. I'd love to show you overpriced restaurants that cater to entitled rich assholes like myself."

"Elliott, that sounds wonderful!"

"But I can't defy Zerby."

"Yes you can! You are more powerful than Zerby!"

And with that she planted a kiss on my lips that caused me to spontaneously manifest a Thanksgiving turkey with corn bread dressing.

Thus our deception began. Under Zerby's watchful eye I kept trying to manifest a carrot, stringing him along by producing beets, yams, rutabagas, Chinese water chestnuts, and other root vegetables.

After Zerby had gone to bed, I quietly manifested tires, fenders, bumpers, bucket seats, and a four-hundred-horsepower engine. This was to be our escape vehicle, a Chevy Corvette that would take Kim and me to freedom.

Kim would take the automotive parts I created and hide them under her bed. In retrospect I was naive, blind to her duplicity and her skill as a mechanic.

The effort to manifest the components of a sports car left me drained of energy, mentally and physically. Kim would come to my cubicle in the wee hours and shed her kimono, but I was too exhausted for lovemaking, and I would drift off to sleep, my thoughts consumed with images of the decoy vegetables I would create the next day.

Finally, after manifesting a hood ornament, it was time for our getaway. I was hastily throwing my belongings into a backpack when Master Zerby burst into my cubicle.

"Where do you think you're going?" he demanded.

"You can't stop us. Kim and I have been planning this for months. We—"

I was cut short by the sound of a revving four-hundred-horse-power engine. Zerby and I ran to the front entrance and looked out.

"Nice car," he said. "I'd love to see it in orange."

"She's leaving without me! She only wanted me for my car!"

"I never allowed her behind the wheel. Her Tibetan driver's license is no good here. If she's pulled over, the publicity will ruin me."

"It would ruin me too," I said, not exactly sure how, but still stinging from Kim's deception.

Zerby rubbed his palms. "If we put our heads together, we can produce—"

"A whole bunch of carrots?"

"Don't be sarcastic. I can be versatile if the situation demands it."

Zerby placed a firm hand on my shoulder.

"Let's make a spike strip."

And that's what we did. As if sharing a single and powerful brain, we visualized a length of metal barbs.

And there on the road, where no spike strip had been before—was a spike strip. In front of Kim's car.

She hit it at ninety miles an hour. Her front tires blew and she went flying over the guard rail, plunging five hundred feet, bursting into a ball of flame, crashing into the valley below.

Tinkle.

* * *

Zerby and I haven't manifested anything since that day, the spike strip having depleted our psychic energy.

Actually, we still have a little energy. We sell homemade preserves at a roadside stand. Zerby manifests the strawberries and I do the mason jars.

And we've opened the magical oriental palace to the public. Anyone seeking a weekend of spiritual perfection is welcome, for two thousand dollars, paid in advance.

Promises of cash manifested at the end of the course will not be accepted.

LET THE PUNISHMENT OF YOUR CHOICE FIT THE CRIME

"All rise," said the bailiff. "Court is now in session. The Honorable Jefferson James Rossiter presiding."

We watched old Judge Rossiter shuffle to the bench, bent forward at a ninety-degree angle. He took his seat and peered down at me.

I had been arrested for forging the names of dead people on checks. Mack Sennett. Ulysses S. Grant. Robin Hood. I had gotten cocky.

"Stanley Finch. Or should I say"—the judge checked his notes—"Jesus of Nazareth."

Like I said, cocky.

"I find you guilty of fraud."

I was cockily acting as my own attorney.

"Have you anything to say, Mr. Finch?"

"Yes, Your Honor. I'd like to apologize to the senior citizens I left impoverished. I'd also like to apologize to Mata Hari and the Incredible Hulk."

"Duly noted," said Judge Rossiter. "Time for the sentencing. What should it be?"

"What should what be?"

"Your sentence."

"You mean . . . I get to pick?"

The judge nodded.

This had to be a test. I hated tests. Tests made me nervous, so I cracked a joke.

"Maybe I should get a rap on the knuckles."

"And why would that be an appropriate punishment?"

"Well, it would probably leave a bruise," I said, wondering how far I could run with this. "Then every time I wrote a bad check, I'd see my black-and-blue knuckles and stop writing, at least until I healed."

"Rap on the knuckles it is," said Judge Rossiter. "Bailiff?"

The muscular bailiff advanced on me. He reached into his shoulder holster, extracted a twelve-inch wooden ruler, and brought it down on my knuckles with a *crack*.

"Ow."

Judge Rossiter nodded. "Let that be a lesson to you. Next case."

That had to be my cue to exit. But I couldn't help it. I lingered.

"That's all? The Catholic grammar school routine?"

"Looked like it smarted. Looks like it's still smarting."

"Well, yes," I said, rubbing the tender spot, "but . . ."

Judge Rossiter waved his hand at me. "Get out of my courtroom."

What was wrong with me? Why was I not making a beeline for the nearest happy hour?

"How can you let a criminal choose? What if I'd picked something even less severe, like a pinch on the forearm?"

"On the fleshy bit by the elbow? Giving it a little twist at the same time? Ouch." The old justice shuddered.

The bailiff began pulling on a black glove.

"No, Bailiff, we're just speculating."

Rossiter motioned for me to come closer.

"Young man, it's been my experience that no one trusts criminals, and that's why they commit crimes. I choose to trust criminals to punish themselves."

"And does that rehabilitate them?"

"I'd like to think it does."

My feet spontaneously performed a short number from *Riverdance*.

"Thank you, Your Honor. You trusted me, and now I don't want to do another crime ever again!"

"You see? It works."

* * *

I sat at a table in the back at Ivan's, a dark smoky bar in the Dark Smoky Bar District. The criminal element hanging out there made Ivan's a dangerous place, as did the smoking.

Across from me was my friend Bob, a.k.a. Bob the Butcher. He was a real-life butcher who decided to start butchering people since he already had the nickname.

You had to know somebody to get into Ivan's, and I was Bob's guest. We'd bonded over our shared interests in crime and collectible Hummel figurines.

"Old Judge Rossiter, eh?" said Bob, straightening his bloody apron and inspecting my bruised knuckles.

"What a monster!" said Bob, suddenly raising his voice so everyone could hear. "Abandon all hope, ye who enter the courtroom of Old-Unnecessarily-Hard-On-Criminals Rossiter!"

"Actually..."

Bob confidentially whispered, "Stanley, I know Rossiter lets you pick your punishment. I've been up before him twice. The first time was after I dismembered a German tourist. The bailiff kicked me in the shins. The second time was for chopping up that Sunday school class."

"And?"

"Bailiff pulled out a nose hair. But we can't broadcast what Judge Rossiter is really like."

My eyes swept around the around the bar, taking in the lawbreakers and their guests.

"Gotcha. If word gets out we'll never get in to see him. He'll be booked for years."

Bob nodded, then resumed a conversational tone. "So I'm wondering if eight hundred dollars is too much to pay for an eleven-inch Merry Wanderer...."

* * *

"Well, Mr. Finch, I see you've moved on from check fraud."

"Yes, Your Honor. Now it's embezzlement, cybercrime, money laundering, and a couple of Ponzi schemes."

Judge Rossiter made a *tsk* sound.

"The evidence is overwhelming. Guilty on all counts."

"I guess I need to be severely punished," I said, suppressing a giggle.

"You do indeed. Fifty years, maximum-security prison."

My heart stopped.

"Ha! Had you goin.'"

"Good one, Your Honor," I said, wiping my sweaty forehead. "Since the financial futures of so many lives have been ruined, I think I should be verbally insulted. Things like bruised knuckles heal over time. But a cutting remark would hurt my feelings forever."

"Well stated, Mr. Finch."

"I took the liberty of writing up a few abusive terms the bailiff could hurl at me."

"I appreciate your initiative," said the judge. The bailiff pouted, disappointed he couldn't make up his own insults. I passed him my list.

"Asshole," muttered the bailiff listlessly. "Dickhead. Idiot. Bed weather."

"That's bed *wetter.*"

"Terrible handwriting," said the bailiff. He gave me back my list.

"Have your feelings been adequately hurt, Mr. Finch?"

"Yes, Your Honor. No more Ponzi schemes for me."

Judge Rossiter solemnly closed his eyes.

I Riverdanced out of the courtroom.

* * *

"And then"—Bob the Butcher's shoulders shook with laughter—"I said I'd give him five hundred dollars for his Apple Tree Boy, but not a penny more. And he took it!"

"An original Apple Tree Boy is worth four grand minimum!"

Bob lowered his voice. "So, Stanley. How about you help me butcher some people?"

I carefully considered my reply. Bob was not just a deranged killer, he was my Hummel buddy, and I didn't want to hurt his feelings.

"I've got a lot on my plate right now . . ."

"It doesn't have to be a big job. We could do a bus."

"A bus?!"

"Not a city bus. A smaller bus, like a rideshare bus."

"Even so . . ."

"You don't have to do any actual butchering. Just hold my cleavers and sharpening steels."

"I wouldn't be comfortable."

"Come on, man. I'm lonely."

"I'm sorry."

"You're not worried about getting caught, are you? Because Judge Rossiter—"

"I've been thinking about Judge Rossiter. I don't think he's doing his job."

"He's doing a *great* job!"

"But I'm still breaking the law. What's more, I'm not enjoying it like I used to. I'm thinking I may have chosen a life of crime because subconsciously I wanted to be punished."

"Okay, you're losing me with the psychology crap. I keep it simple. All I need is a cleaver, a victim, and a chance to do it again tomorrow."

I rose from the table.

"I need to back off for a while," I said.

"Cleaver and a victim," Bob repeated, "and once in a while a deal on a Benevolent Birdfeeder."

* * *

"All rise," said the bailiff. "The Honorable Jefferson James Rossifer presiding."

I snickered. "I think you mean *Rossiter*."

I could tell the bailiff still held a grudge about not getting to make up his own insults. "This is Judge *Rossifer*," he sneered. "Totally different guy."

Judge Rossifer looked like Judge Rossiter in the way all old white men look alike. But this old white man had crooked teeth and a broken nose and a long purple scar on his left cheek, making it easier to tell him apart from other judges.

"There's been a mistake," I blurted.

"There has indeed, young man," said Judge Rossifer, drooling, another feature that set him apart.

"I should be in front of Judge Rossiter. Can I have my regular judge now, please?"

"Judge Rossiter doesn't handle jaywalking."

"Oh, all right," I sighed, turning to the bailiff. "Pinch my right earlobe. Don't pull and don't twist. Just pinch it hard for two seconds."

"I have a better idea," said Judge Rossifer. "How about you spend thirty days in the county jail?"

"I'd prefer an earlobe pinch."

"I don't care what you'd prefer. I'm the judge!" he shouted. "Sixty days in county jail."

"No. I get to pick."

"Not in my court you don't!" He pounded the bench with his fists. "I'm fed up being confused with Judge Pushover. Today it stops!"

Judge Rossifer pointed a finger at me.

"One year in federal prison," he drooled.

"Now you're being ridiculous."

"No!" said Judge Rossifer, standing up on shaky legs. "Ridiculous is a mugger getting a spanking. An arsonist being sent to bed early. A serial killer standing in the corner for ten minutes. I sentence you to fifty years in maximum-security prison."

"That was funnier when Judge Rossiter said it."

"You're going to prison because of the others of your ilk who let themselves off easy."

"You're punishing other criminals by punishing *me*?"

"You got it."

"But that's . . ."

I stopped. All that confusion I had, wondering if I committed crimes so I'd be caught . . . all that vanished. For the first time in years I felt good. I felt like I was making a contribution.

I looked up at the judge. "Can I pick my cell?"

"No."

"Can my uniform be burgundy?"

"No. You don't get to pick anything anymore."

I nodded. "That's how it should be."

Two police officers seized me before I could do a hornpipe.

* * *

I spent the next couple months in prison writing cards to the criminals who had let themselves off easy. I wanted them to know I was taking the heat for them. There were cartoon storks on the cards, because birth announcements were all I could get.

"Here's the next batch," I said to Bob the Butcher as I slid the stamped cards across the table.

"The guys at Ivan's are all really proud of you for what you're doing," said Bob.

"It's my pleasure," I said. "I'm sleeping with a clear conscience."

"We all chipped in and got you this."

Bob placed a box on the table. I opened it and unwrapped the tissue paper.

"Aww. A Hummel Little Fiddler. I'm touched."

"Well," said Bob, standing. "I'm off. Tonight it's a barber-shop quartet."

"Singing?"

"Slaughtering."

I shrugged. "Might as well. I've got your debt to society covered."

"And don't for a minute think I'm not grateful. Bye, Stanley."

"Bye, Bob."

INSTRUCTIONS FOR MY DAILY FUNERAL

Make the first one traditional. Small chapel. Tasteful floral arrangements. Classical organ music. (I don't know any classical music, so you pick). Open casket. No need to dress me in a fancy suit, that would be a waste. Just bury me in a Brioni embroidered floral dinner jacket.

It won't be me in the casket, obviously. It's a lookalike. A really good lookalike, so everyone who knew me in life will be fooled. If you can't get a really good lookalike, close the lid. Of course if the lid is closed, there's no need for a lookalike. Get any old dead body—what am I saying? Put in a sack of potatoes. That would be more respectful of human life, plus you'd save money on the Brioni jacket.

Where will I be? In the front row. Best seat in the house. I'll be in disguise, unrecognizable, as a British lord in a bowler hat, with a monocle. Guests will mutter, "We knew he was important, but we didn't realize he knew a British lord who resembles him." I will bite the tip of my British sword cane to suppress my laughter.

Helen Mirren should deliver my eulogy. I want my eulogy read by a real celebrity, not a celebrity lookalike, that's just for in the casket. I'm not picky. I'll settle for any celebrity—famous actor, supermodel, sports superstar. It doesn't have to be Helen Mirren, I just thought of her because I have England on my mind. Try Helen first.

For the second funeral, we can loosen things up. Have some fun. Hold it in a planetarium or a pizza parlor. Polka music. Me in the casket, dressed in a flannel onesie with dinosaurs on it. And when I say "me," of course, I mean a new lookalike, since the guy from yesterday will be ashes.

This point deserves clarification. After every funeral, the body should be cremated. I'm not going to pay for full-size cemetery plots, not if I also have to pay Helen Mirren.

Make sure the lookalikes know they'll be cremated, before they agree to take the job—that's common courtesy. Get them to sign a release, and if they balk, threaten their families.

I'll still be in the front row as a British lord, only with a monocle in the opposite eye, in case anyone's there from the day before.

I don't want to put words in Helen Mirren's mouth, or the mouth of whatever celebrity we get, but here are some suggestions:

He was great man.

He performed great deeds.

He led a great life, greater even than Catherine the Great, who I played in a television miniseries.

While any celebrity could say these words, they would be most effective spoken by Helen Mirren.

You may be wondering what's in this for me. I'll tell you. I hope that, in death, I'll be fondly remembered, because let's face it, right now everyone thinks I'm an asshole—which is why it's important for me to be nice to the lookalikes who are about to die.

We can really blow it out with the subsequent funerals. You're gonna need a new crowd every day. Offer free beer.

In certain cultures, I understand they have professional mourners. Let's do that. I would like the mourners to be female, between the ages of 20 and 29, in glittery costumes, wailing and performing tight choreography. Perhaps you can get the Rockettes, if they're not too busy rehearsing their Christmas Spectacular.

If the same female mourners could be my pallbearers too, that would be cool, especially if they danced on the way to the crematorium.

What do we do with the ashes? We'll bury them in little graves, smaller than big expensive casket holes, and marked by gravestones scattered all over the cemetery, so as not to arouse suspicion. Or maybe just have one big gravestone, where the date of death keeps rolling over like a clock radio.

We could also scatter the ashes, which would be a thoughtful gesture to the families of the cremated lookalikes. But people can have crazy ideas about how they want their ashes scattered, like from a balloon or a submarine, and that creates needless paperwork, so forget it.

Each time, I'll be there in disguise: as a Mexican lord in a sombrero, a Turkish lord in a fez, an Arabian lord in a keffiyeh, an African lord in a kufi cap, or maybe just a monocle salesman, if I don't feel like wearing a hat.

Let's keep getting bigger and better celebrities. I realize the President of the United States is a busy man, so if he wants to prerecord his eulogy, that's fine.

There's always food after a funeral, and I'm really looking forward to that. The menu ought not to give away my disguise, so don't serve British food if I'm a British lord, or Mexican food if I'm a Mexican lord—wait, maybe you *should* serve the same food as my disguise, and then I'll comment on the remarkable coincidence. Let's try it both ways.

Afterward, go ahead, read my will. But don't give away my stuff until I'm really dead, because I might need it.

The daily funerals should continue until I actually die. When I'm finally dead, who needs a funeral if I'm not there to see it. Leave my body in a broken refrigerator by the side of the road, for all I care.

That covers everything. Let's get started. Time for me to be fondly remembered.

By the way, if Helen Mirren wants to prerecord her eulogy, I'm also fine with that.

PICK A BLISS, ANY BLISS

I was losing my hair. Every day there were clumps on my hairbrush, in the bathtub drain, on my pillow, sometimes in my breakfast. It had to be my hair because I live alone.

The hair-loss expert I was seeing—Louis Cantilever, an expensive follicle savant with an eponymous line of hair-restoration products and a luxurious mane of his own—sat at his desk and opened my file.

"Dale Crab."

"Yes."

"It's no wonder you're not getting results. You've only spent two thousand dollars." He gestured to the dozen or so bottles on his desk, each one with his hairy pate on the label. "You should try the Cantilever Energizing Conditioner in the Waterford Crystal decanter."

"I've been thinking," I said. "My hair loss may be due to psychological factors. I should probably see a therapist."

I felt the breeze as he shook his locks back and forth.

"Don't be hasty. You're off to a great start. Another two thousand dollars and you'll look as good as me."

"I'm gonna see a therapist."

I made an appointment and put Luke in charge while I was gone. Luke was raw ambition with a pimply face. As much as I hated him, I knew he could run my Burger Clown franchise while I was out.

The therapist was an attractive woman ten years younger than myself, like I needed another reason to be ashamed of my encroaching baldness. What was worse, she never told me her first name and insisted I call her Dr. Klein. That shouldn't have bothered me, but it did.

"Why don't you take off your baseball cap and tell me what's going on with you?"

I put my cap in my lap.

"Well, as you can see, I'm losing my hair. I'm wondering if it's psychological."

"Let's explore that. How are you feeling about your life right now?"

Where to start?

"I'm feeling right now... like my life sucks. I've managed a Burger Clown franchise for eighteen years, and I hate it. I hate my employees. I hate pizza-face Luke and Renee with her pierced lips and her neck tattoo. I hate the smell of french fry grease. Luke and Renee smell like french fry grease and so do the orange booths and so do the fat customers after they've been sitting in the booths stuffing their fat faces."

I gagged a little as I remembered the smell of french fry grease and the neck tattoo.

"Mm-hm," said Dr. Klein smoothly. "If I might make a suggestion . . ."

She uncrossed and crossed her pretty legs. The exposed skin on the top of my skull was burning.

"Have you ever heard of Joseph Campbell?"

"The soup guy?"

"No. Literature professor. He said, 'Follow your bliss.'"

"What does that mean?"

"It means, do whatever satisfies your soul in the deepest possible way."

"So should I fire Luke and Renee?"

"Deeper than that."

"Then what is my bliss?"

"I can't tell you."

Uncross. Cross. I put my cap back on to hide the sweat.

"If you can't, who can?"

"No one. You must find it yourself."

"Just tell me. Money is no object."

"Dale, please."

"When I find my bliss, will my hair grow back?"

"Our session is over."

Follow my bliss. But first, find it. Where to start?

The dictionary said bliss was "'perfect happiness, great joy." But firing Luke and Renee didn't count. This was really hard.

Thinking about bliss exhausted me, and I had to take a nap. Just before I fell asleep, a memory bubbled up from my subconscious. I was standing in line at Bed Bath & Beyond, waiting to pay for a potato peeler. That's where I saw it hanging on the wall in the art section: a framed poster of a guy on a mountaintop with his arms raised to heaven. Superimposed over his image were the words FOLLOW YOUR BLISS.

I knew then what I had to do. I had to buy that poster. No, I'm kidding. I had to climb a mountain.

My rock-climbing guide was Rick Frendo, upbeat and fit, and when I asked if rock climbing was a way to follow your bliss he said,

"Dude, absolutely. It is one hundred percent my bliss." Rick was ten years younger than myself, like Dr. Klein, with possibly even prettier legs.

When the big day arrived for the climb, I was scared, but I knew that very soon I would be raising my arms in the air just like poster guy. Rick Frendo calmed me, saying, "Don't worry, dude, I've got your back."

He got not only my back but my front and arms and legs too. When we were ten feet off the ground, I went rigid with terror, like I had rigor mortis. Rick carried me up the remaining 180 feet. At the summit my body unfroze. Rick said, "Dude," which I think meant "Look at the view."

I took in the incredible vista stretching for miles, but it didn't move me like I hoped it would. A couple of hairs from my head fluttered away in the wind. My arms did not spontaneously raise, and I thought maybe if I forced them to go up I would feel blissful. Unfortunately Rick was standing too close, and as I lifted my arms I accidentally punched him in the jaw, causing him to fall backward off the mountain.

The disappointing view, and the sound of Rick Frendo screaming, made me realize his bliss was not mine.

Maybe somebody else had a better bliss for me, a bliss that didn't involve sheer rock faces.

I remembered how good I felt whenever I received an act of kindness. Gestures as small as a smile and a "How are you?" could make my day. I longed for simple demonstrations of warmth, demonstrations I never got from Luke the Tool or Renee the Pus Bag.

That could be my bliss. Receiving kindness from those around me. But where could I find it?

There was a Red Cross office near the Burger Clown. The office had a sign in the window that read, VOLUNTEERS NEEDED. The Red Cross was kind, right? I entered, eager to receive kindness.

The East Indian lady behind the front desk was nice and I'm sure a great giver of kindness.

"Are you here to volunteer, sir?"

"Yes," I said, "I'm here to volunteer to be the recipient of kindness."

She cocked her head in a kind but confused way.

"I want to follow my bliss. I think if people were kind and considerate to me, that could be my bliss."

She nodded as if she understood.

"Our volunteers find that the more kindness they give to the poor and the sick, the more kindness is returned to them."

"What are you saying? I have to do it first?"

"Yes, sir."

"And how long before people start being kind to me?"

"It can happen almost immediately."

She was wrong. It didn't happen immediately. It didn't happen at all. I don't know how many hours I wasted smiling at the sick and the poor, saying, "How are you?" and then waiting for them to be kind back to me. Most of the sick ones were too sick to even sit up, never mind being kind. And the poor ones seemed like they always wanted something more—money or food or shoes or housing or I don't know what.

I was working at the Red Cross soup kitchen one day, serving lunch to the poor, noticing my hair falling into the tuna noodle casserole, thinking this was worse than Burger Clown because I wasn't making a cent. Having had enough I shouted, "No more food for anybody until you make me feel good!"

My fellow volunteers were shocked. Mandy, the young woman next to me, scolded, "Don't be selfish."

"I'm just trying to follow my bliss."

"Well, so am I."

"Ha! How's that working out for you?"

"It's working perfectly. Simply knowing that I've made these people's lives a little easier is enough for me."

"You think they'll ever feed you like you're feeding them?"

"Probably not. That doesn't matter."

"I'm sorry, Mandy, but that's a one-sided bliss," I said, removing my apron. "Nothing here makes me want to raise my arms to heaven like this." I lifted my ladle over my head. "I'm outta here."

As I exited, the other volunteers and the poor people shouted profanity-laden variations of "Good riddance." Hey, Red Cross? Next time there's a hurricane I'll provide my own boat, thank you.

I thought I should give the mountain one more chance. It could be that before, I faced the wrong way, and missed a more incredible vista behind me. But Rick Frendo, with several pins in his legs, made sure his mountain-climbing friends knew my name, so nobody would carry me up the rock face.

I gave up. Finding your bliss was for other people, not me. I resigned myself to being a blissless bald manager of a fast-food restaurant until I croaked.

But when I returned to work, and opened the door, and got hit with that old familiar smell, a name popped into my head:

Joseph Campbell.

Dr. Klein said "follow your bliss" was his invention.

If anybody could tell me what my bliss was and help prevent hair loss, it was Joseph Campbell.

In my haste to find him I overlooked the fact that he was dead. Instead, I ended up at the front door of a Joe Campbell in Naperville, Illinois.

"I want to follow my bliss, but I don't know what it is. I need you to help me find it. In exchange I will do anything for you."

Joe scratched the beer belly protruding from under his soiled tank top.

"Okay," he said. "Get me a pack of smokes."

I got him his smokes. I also got him a turkey sandwich and a six-pack of Coors Light.

Then I washed his windows. I fixed a hole in his screen door. I cleaned the leaves out of his gutters.

All the time Joe Campbell swore he was thinking about my bliss.

It was like Mr. Miyagi making Ralph Macchio do "wax on, wax off," in *The Karate Kid*, except on Joe Campbell's car there were no spots to wax because of all the rust.

I cleaned out his septic tank. I installed dormer windows. I built a cedar pergola that covered his patio in back.

Joe Campbell kept thinking.

There was nothing I wouldn't have done for him. I had "bliss blindness," and if that's not a medical term, it ought to be.

Then one day, as I was sealing the cracks in his blacktop driveway, I noticed something exciting. There were no stray hairs in the wet blacktop sealant. I wasn't losing them anymore.

And I got it. Do something for somebody else. Simple selfless service. That was my bliss.

The Red Cross had the right idea. But I didn't really get it until I was doing things for Joe Campbell.

I shook Joe's hand and thanked him for showing me the light, something all those poor people were unable to do.

"I now know what my bliss is. Simple selfless service."

"My bathtub needs recaulking."

"Bye, Joe." I extracted my hand and hurried away.

My hair didn't grow back, but it didn't fall out anymore either.

I called Luke and Renee into my office. The odor of french fries preceded them.

"From now on," I said, "our new motto at Burger Clown is 'simple selfless service.'"

"So . . . do we give away free milkshakes?" said Luke.

"Do we add extra fries to their orders?" said Renee.

"Not necessarily."

"Because you can't make money if you give away free stuff," said Luke, wrinkling his brow, giving the matter serious thought.

"I'm aware of that. What I'm talking about is an attitude that says, my ego is less important than your needs."

Vacant stares.

"It's my bliss," I declared, thrusting my arms in the air.

Vacant stares with open mouths. The redolence of french fry grease.

"Get out of my office."

TODAY'S SPECIAL: RAGGLE WITH A BOOM STICK

You could call it The Promised Land. But it wasn't a land, it was a table. So, The Promised Table. That's what it was to me.

Private detectives had their own table at the Greek's Greek Deli and Greek Restaurant, owned by a Swede who dyed his hair black so he could look Greek.

When they weren't private detecting, the Detectives' Table was where you'd find the trio.

Sam always had a cigarette between his lips. He could smoke it without touching it. He could also light it without using a match, then walk to the newsstand and buy a fresh pack without using money or his feet. I worshipped him.

Jake's nose had been slashed by a mean little gangster. Jake thought his nose was hanging on by a thread. But clearly it wasn't, it had been completely sliced off his face. No one had the heart to tell him, that's how much everyone admired Jake.

Phil . . . well, Phil was Phil. He'd seen it all.

One day, it finally happened. It was Tuesday, late morning. Jake waved me over to sit at the Detectives' Table, using the hand he wasn't using to hold on his nose. The three of them had probably spotted me sitting at the counter in my trench coat and fedora, staring at them for the past, I don't know, two or three years.

I leaped up from my stool and tried to look composed as I skipped over to them.

"Derek Organ," I said, sitting down.

"Sam."

"Jake."

"Phil, not that it matters in this ugly old whore of a town."

"Man, that's profound."

The renown of these detectives was reflected in the menu. Each guy had a dish named after him: The Sam, The Jake, The Not-That-It-Matters Phil—three different names for a Denver omelette. I ordered one of each, as a show of respect.

"Don't let me interrupt," I said with a mouth full of my first Denver.

"I was telling these dicks about my last case," said Sam, as he caused a lit cigarette to appear out of his nose. "So this raggle storms into my office and pulls a boom stick out of her clutch."

"No foolin'? That the same Zelda who was hitched to the bruno?" said Phil.

"Nah," said Jake, "he's talking about the biscuit with the deuce."

"Oh, her."

"Right," said Sam.

"I know exactly what you mean," I said. "And I know exactly what a bruno is."

"Good for you," said Phil out of the side of his mouth.

"But just to be clear," I said as I tried to swallow a chunk of ham, "what size bruno was it? Large? Small?"

"Average-sized bruno," said Sam through clenched teeth.

"Right. What color bruno? Solid? Or maybe a pattern?"

Three pairs of eyes stared at me. Jake laid his nose on the table so he could give full attention to his stare.

"He doesn't know what the hell you're talking about," said Phil to Sam.

"Come on, of course I know what you're talking about. I'm a detective, just like you guys."

Sam and Phil shook their heads. Jake replaced his nose on his face so he could snort through it.

I began to sweat. I had to say something to save face, not an easy task with a mouthful of egg.

"A razzle . . . had a broomstick . . . and was eating a Triscuit . . . with the Duke . . ."

Silence, except for my chewing sounds.

Nice recovery, I said to myself, starting on my second omelette.

* * *

"Hey guys, my chair is missing," I said to my three new friends when I returned from the men's room. Then I realized that, because they were detectives, they had probably already noticed the missing furniture. Nothing got past them.

"So what happened to my chair, Sam?"

Sam shrugged without using his shoulders.

"Do you know, Jake?"

"I haven't seen your chair, Organ. I've been too busy holding my nose on my face," said Jake, unaware he was holding it upside down.

Phil, in his worldly way, was playing with the pieces of the broken chair right in front of me, making a little log cabin out of the legs.

"Phil, is that my broken chair?"

"Does it matter?"

"Well, yes, it—"

"It doesn't matter to me. This town is an ugly old whore."

By now I was pretty sure they'd broken my chair and were letting Phil play with the pieces. Hell, I was a detective too.

"Was it something I said?"

* * *

They didn't boot me out of the deli. They did something worse. They made me sit at the kids' table.

The yellow plastic table in the corner rose to a height of no less than eighteen inches. Four chairs in primary colors stood at each side. The red and orange chairs held two little girls in party dresses and paper crowns. I dropped down onto a blue chair, bending the legs nearly to the floor. I'm happy to say the legs on the green chair were bent even farther to the floor by a chubby kid in a tight striped t-shirt.

Sure, I could have simply exited the Greek Restaurant with whatever was left of my dignity—but that would have seemed to the detectives like I was accepting failure.

"Don't you think that would have seemed like I was accepting failure?" I said to Chubby.

"You're stupid," he said.

"No, you're stupid," I replied.

"No, you."

"No, you."

"We're princesses," said one of the two little girls.

"And you're in our kingdom," said the other.

"Your kingdom is an ugly old whore," I said, winking across the room at Phil. But he couldn't see me and I couldn't see him; all I could see were his socks under the table. World-weary socks. Socks that saw corruption lurking everywhere, behind the facade of respectable power. Phil's socks were my hero.

I had no idea who these kids belonged to. But I wished their parents would come and pick them up soon, so I could have all the crayons and drawing paper to myself.

Service at the kids' table was dreadful. I mean, how long does it take to make a teddy bear pancake?

When, after an hour, the waiter finally brought our food—the princesses wanted to leave a nickel tip but I talked them out of it—I discovered I was no longer hungry. I stared into the chocolate chip eyes of the pancake bear.

"If you don't finish your pancake," said the bossier of the two girls, "you can't come to the ball."

"All my life," I said, close to tears, "I wanted to be a private detective. And to be rejected by those guys, my heroes—I can't imagine anything worse."

Chubby looked at me with a mouthful of chicken tenders.

"Get over it," he said. "I heard everything they said. They were testing you. You think they're going to hand you their respect on a silver platter. So they threw some private dick jargon at you. So they took away your chair. So what?"

"Grow a pair," said the princesses in unison.

I didn't want the other people in the restaurant to know I was taking advice from children, so I eased out of my chair and crawled under the table. Chubby was already there.

"I hate to admit it, but you're right," I said to the little porker. "Funny thing is, I think I'd respect those guys less if they admitted me into their inner circle without a struggle. You're onto something . . . You've got chicken tender on your chin."

"You're stupid," said Chubby.

"No, you're stupid."

"No, you."

"No, you."

"No, you."

"I have to go pee-pee," I said, and excused myself.

* * *

When I returned from making pee-pee—a good pee-pee, one of my best—my blue plastic chair was missing.

As a rule I'm reluctant to accuse little girls of theft. But while I was gone, my tablemates had somehow acquired a blue plastic castle filled with blue plastic lords and ladies. The smell of melted blue plastic permeated the air.

"I know when I'm not wanted," I said.

"No you don't," said Chubby.

"Yes I do. I'm not stupid."

"Yes you are."

I refused to get into another pointless exchange with Chubby.

"NOT NOT NOT NOT NOT NOT NOT!" I screamed, then bolted out of the restaurant.

* * *

Back in my office, I had plenty of time to think. Business was slow—okay, nonexistent. There were no razzles with broomsticks in my waiting room. No Triscuit-eating Dukes either.

My mind kept going over the words Chubby had said to me: "No you, no you, no you . . . " Eventually my mind tired of those words and moved on to his other, better words: "They were testing you . . . you think they're going to hand you their respect on a silver platter? . . ."

Of course! I was already sitting bolt upright, but I slouched so I could sit bolt upright again. Of course! Two could play at this "testing" game. Or three. Or even better, four. That way I'd be included . . .

* * *

I strode through the doors of the Greek's Greek Restaurant, a man on a mission. The trio was still there at the Detectives' Table. They looked smaller to me, and sadder. Jake's nose, which he still insisted was attached to his face, had shriveled and blackened like a rotten plum.

Sam had quit cigarettes and was now smoking celery sticks, which in my opinion looked less sophisticated.

Phil was poring over a map of the United States, looking for a different dirty old whore of a city for a weekend getaway.

Uninvited, I pushed a La-Z-Boy recliner up to the Detectives' Table and settled into the soft cushions. I had a story to tell, and I was going to tell it in maximum comfort.

"Not so good at taking a hint, are you, Organ?" sneered Sam through a haze of celery smoke.

"So the other day," I said, ignoring him, "I'm in my office, minding my own business . . . when this parachute slithers in. Let me tell you, her chipmunks were primed for teatime."

That got their attention.

"As you can imagine, I was feeling hyperbolic, so much so that I failed to notice a barnacle slip in the door behind her."

The trio leaned forward, enthralled. I snatched one of Sam's celery sticks and fired it up.

"Big mistake on my part. Next thing you know I've got a chandelier where my bamboo cocktail toothpick should be."

They nodded. They bought it. I settled deeper into the recliner. I was one happy dick.

Sam, Jake, and Phil exchanged a look, then burst into laughter. Jake laughed so hard he shot orange juice out his nose, using a three-foot rubber tube.

"You had us going, Organ," said Phil.

"Call me Derek."

"No."

"Okay."

"You sure turned the tables on us, Organ," said Sam.

"Would *you* like to call me Derek?"

"No, never."

"Okay."

"You're smart," said Sam. "You used a sort of word salad to show how we get too proprietary with our private dick lingo."

"Sometimes I think we keep ourselves too isolated," mused Phil, "by using words only we understand."

"Even *I* don't understand half the things we say," said Jake. "What's a boom stick again?"

"A blackjack," said Sam.

"I thought it was dynamite," said Phil.

"It doesn't matter," said Sam. "Organ, lose that recliner, get a normal diner chair, and have another celery stick. You're welcome at the Detectives' Table anytime."

I sniffed.

"You think it's that easy to make nice with Derek Organ?" I told them. "Sorry, pals. Phil, you said you three were too isolated. Well, you're a hundred twenty percent correct. I don't need to be a part of your tiny world. I am Derek Organ, Private Detective, and I'm a citizen of the world. Adios, mugs!"

* * *

"No, you!"

"No, you!"

"No, you!"

"No, you!"

I was wearing a tiara and a backless dress with puffy sleeves. If I didn't wear the dress, the princesses wouldn't let me back at their table.

I had no idea how our argument started. But there was no way I'd let Chubby gain the upper hand.

"No, you!"

"No, you! . . ."

DIARY OF A MAD STOCK BOY

MAY 15

Am I mad? Others have thought so. I don't believe I am. But you decide. Hear my story and then ask yourself: Can any man who converses with snack food be truly mad?

My name is Warren P. Tungsten, and I'm a sixty-two-year-old supermarket stock boy. My wife, Jill, refuses to face up to this truth. She continues to think of me as Warren P. Tungsten, sixty-two-year-old insurance claims adjustor. Many is the time we've exchanged heated words on the topic.

I've repeatedly explained to her it's important I spend the few precious years I have left to me making it easy for shoppers to find the colorfully packaged processed American foods they require. I was nourished by these products in my youth, and now I wish to give back. (I ought not to play favorites, but I am especially fond of the snacks in aisle nine.)

Will Jill insist I keep my job as a claims adjuster, with a salary ten times greater than that of a stock boy? Will she accept my higher calling in the supermarket? Will she find the aprons I have hidden from her?

* * *

MAY 17

"Where are you hiding your aprons? I thought I burned them all!" Jill screams at me as she waves a blowtorch in the air. Fortunately, today I had the foresight to wear my apron under my clothes. Jill is foolish. She thinks by burning my aprons she'll prevent me from showing up at the supermarket. But I'd work in a burnt and blackened apron, that's how dedicated I am. My boss, Angel, might not be thrilled, but he'd forgive me. Angel is a good kid, forty years my junior. If I had a son, I'd want him to be just like Angel—wait, I *do* have a son. I forgot.

"Stan called," says Jill testily.

"Is Stan my son?"

"No, Stan is your boss at Consolidated Insurance."

"Oh, right."

I would never want Stan as a son. He's not a good kid. He's not a kid at all.

"Stan is waiting for your report on the supper-club fire," reports Jill.

"I'm sure it's a legitimate claim, as are most mob-owned supper-club fires. Now if you'll excuse me, the snack aisle is calling."

I push past Jill and head for the door, as Jill falls to her knees, weeping, again. She will never understand. Insurance claims adjustment pays the bills. But it's boring work, for boring men with dull minds. I'd rather unload sacks of Doritos.

* * *

MAY 30

We receive an out-of-the-ordinary delivery today. I don't trust the size of the truck. Most of our grocery deliveries come in massive 18-wheelers, friendly American behemoths packed with sugary breakfast cereals and processed lunch meats. This was a van. It didn't deserve to kiss the hem of an 18-wheeler's garment.

"Angel, that van is too small to be trusted. I also don't trust the painting on the side, the one of the cow with the beret and the word *fromage* underneath."

"It's French."

"Oh, really? Is it really French? Well, pardon *moi* while I go laugh at a Jerry Lewis movie."

"Stop being sarcastic and start unloading. We're setting up a gourmet cheese section."

"We already have a cheese section."

"*Gourmet*, Warren," Angel said, implying that in the brave new cheese section he envisioned, there would be no place for individually wrapped American slices.

* * *

Mimolette. That's what the cheese was called. It came in wedges, sliced from a big ball. A big ball of French cheese. Also it was orange, a haughty orange, not a friendly orange like a Cheeto.

"Make sure Mimolette is prominently featured."

You mean the *Mimolette*, I think. We're talking about a cheese, not a French schoolgirl.

Angel walks away, clearly smitten. I wear rubber gloves as I arrange the display of *the* Mimolette, along with the Eiffel Towers, the Charles de Gaulles, whatever the hell those other French cheeses are. As I place the Mimolette in the center of the case and turn my back, I swear that little *fromage* sniffs at me in a derogatory way, expressing displeasure at my arrangement skills. I ignore it. I'm better than that.

After stocking for forty-five minutes, I can't breathe. I duck into a stall in the employees' restroom for some fresh air. The odor in there is nothing compared to the *fromage* stench permeating my clothes. I flush my apron and get a fresh one from my locker. I have a little more work to do, stocking aged François Truffaut or something.

I return to the gourmet cheese display. It's quiet, the quiet of a room suddenly becoming silent because everyone was talking about you. You could cut the tension with a knife, a cheese knife or any other knife. And you didn't have to be an expert on talking French cheeses to know who had been instigating the gossip.

"What?" says Angel in his office.

"I'm saying the French cheeses don't like me. And that little princess is the ringleader."

"That's crazy talk, Warren."

Right, I think. *And you have the hots for a dairy product.*

I take the afternoon off.

* * *

MAY 31—2:00 A.M.

"Please come to bed, Warren, darling," says Jill as I pace around our bedroom. She's trying to be affectionate, but her blowtorch is on the nightstand.

"I've created a balanced ecosystem," I explain patiently. "Every aisle a model of peaceful coexistence. Then along comes this foreigner who thinks she's better than other foods, and better than me too."

I pull my apron on over my pajamas.

"I won't take it lying down." I feel the pocket of my apron to make sure I have my key to the supermarket door, then hurry out of the bedroom.

"Warren, please," Jill calls out. "You're totally self-absorbed."

"What? No, I'm not."

"Yes, you are. Even your daughter says so."

"I have a daughter?"

* * *

MAY 31—8:00 A.M.

When I arrive at the store the next morning, Angel meets me at the entrance, tears streaming down his cheeks.

"How could such a thing happen?" he says, as I follow him to aisle nine. There is the Mimolette, or what's left of her—a tiny pile of orange crumbles on the floor.

On the shelves, ridged potato chips look the other way. Mixed nuts whistle nonchalantly. Beef jerky pretends to be absorbed in today's newspaper.

I shake my head, mustering up a display of sympathy. "It's unfortunate. But clearly the French cheese—"

"Mimolette. She has a name."

"Clearly *the* Mimolette wandered into an unfriendly snack section."

"She doesn't have legs. Somebody put her here. Was it you? You hated her from the start."

"Come on. You can't hate a cheese."

"If you can love a cheese, you can hate a cheese."

Angel wipes his tears on his sleeve.

"Please clean her up. Respectfully."

This wasn't what I wanted. I'd entered the store at night. I picked her up and dropped her there in aisle nine, thinking if she rubbed elbows with common American snacks, she'd get over herself. How was I to know she was incapable of getting over herself? How was I to know they'd react with such vehemence?

Actually, maybe this *is* what I wanted.

* * *

JUNE 2

I lie in bed, next to Jill, musing.

"That cheese I thought was the Eiffel Tower? It's actually Reblochon. I googled it."

"Stan from Consolidated Insurance called again today. He said you're fired."

"The other cheeses are Chevrotin, Trou du Cru . . ."

"Please stop saying cheese names."

"Brillat-Savarin, Crottin de Chavignol. I can smell them at fifty paces."

"You're a terrible provider. And you're insane. I'm leaving you. And I'm taking Jessica and Tyler."

"I bet those are my kids."

* * *

JUNE 3—8:00 A.M.

Angel once again meets me at the entrance. He isn't crying. I'm worried.

He leads me to aisle nine.

Something has gone terribly wrong.

There on the shelves, amid my beloved pork rinds and Chex Mix, are the French cheeses. I'm struck dumb. The snacks and the cheeses have their arms around each other. (I believe I'm the only one who can see this.) They are also singing. (I believe I'm the only one who can hear this.) Their song goes:

Doesn't matter if we're runny,

doesn't matter if we're stale.

Everybody loves us

with a glass of wine or ale.

Yes, everybody loves us

more than kale.

Curse these foreigners with their phlegmy accents and their catchy anthems.

"I know it was you who moved the cheeses, Warren. You broke in after midnight—"

"I have a key."

"I guess you were hoping for violence, like with Mimolette."

It's true. I'm too disappointed to deny it, as I look at the spotless floor where I hoped to find a greasy smear of Jacques Cousteau.

"Turn in your apron. You're fired."

I chuckle to myself, knowing I have a dozen aprons at home and another fifty in storage.

Before I leave, I look at my old friends—the potato chips and the pretzel rods and the others. They pretended not to recognize me. Of course they'd respond to the bonhomie of the French cheeses. They're food, and I'm a person.

For the first time, the gulf between us seems insurmountable.

JUNE 24

More than getting back my job, more than reuniting with Jill and my children—Janice and Toby, I think they're called—I need to convince the snacks that I am their true friend, not these Gallic douchebags.

I have a plan. I will meet my friends on their level, snack to snack.

A disguise is required. I will present myself as a new product on the market called Señor Munch, crispy potato goodness with a hint of jalapeño. It will be a simple matter to create colorful man-size cellophane packaging, now that the house is empty and I'm free to work in any room I choose.

* * *

JUNE 25

For a time, it seemed my plan would succeed. In the wee hours I let myself into the store with a spare key—I have as many spare keys as I have spare aprons. I lie down in aisle nine, unable to stock myself, but confident that whoever my replacement is will place me on the shelf and I can begin reconciliation.

The following morning Angel fails to recognize me, so effective is my Señor Munch disguise. However, because I'm a new, he decides I should have a display all my own. Paulie, my replacement, a skinny kid with a lazy eye, places me on a rack near the checkout line.

And here I sit, alone. Soon I will tear off the cellophane and walk away. But . . .

I see a family of nine approaching, attracted by two factors: the bright colors of my getup, and my size. No doubt they're thinking about the money they'll save by buying Señor Munch in bulk.

I can do this. I can feed them. I can nourish them. I guess deep down I was always a snack.

I remain in my rack.

STUCK IN AN ELEVATOR PLAY

The elevator lurched to a stop between the twenty-seventh and twenty-eighth floors.

"Yikes!" said Danielle, looking cute in a white blouse and navy blue skirt. I saw this as an opportunity to impress her with my take-charge attitude.

"Don't panic. I've been stuck on elevators before and believe me, this is nothing compared to a bungee jump. Remember I told you I did a bungee jump in Los Cabos?"

"Who are you again?"

"Tom."

"Tom Truffalo?"

"Tom Eigerdell."

"In the cubicle by the kitchen?"

"No, the one by the men's room."

"Tom Truffalo went skydiving in Spain."

"Everybody does that," I said dismissively.

Somehow my plan to impress her ended up with a discussion of Spanish skydiving. I wouldn't let that happen again, next time we were trapped in an elevator or a fire or earthquake.

As I reached for the red button on the console to call maintenance, a guy with piercing green eyes and a manicured red beard grabbed my wrist.

"Wait," he said. "If we're rescued now, it will interfere with my process."

Okay, that sounded like Urdu or some other made-up language.

"You're the new temp."

"Only temporarily," he said, winking at Danielle. She giggled, I'm sorry to say.

"In real life I'm a playwright," said Red Beard. "My name is Grayberg Starchmont."

I wish Danielle had giggled at his stupid name instead of his stupid temp joke.

"Written any movies I might have seen?" I asked him.

Starchmont stared at me.

"Playwrights write plays, not movies," said Danielle, suddenly an expert on plays and movies.

I'd lost control, like with Spanish skydiving. I had to find a way to make Danielle panic again, so I could regain the upper hand.

"We'd better call somebody before we start eating each other," I said.

She didn't panic. In fact she took offense. Maybe she had relatives who were cannibals.

The elevator felt smaller. It was smellier too, because I'd farted from stress.

"What do you mean when you say your 'process'?" Danielle asked Starchmont, putting herself between me and the red alarm button.

"It's as if my ideas are embryos, suspended in the ether, waiting for me to welcome them, to birth them." He waved his hands in the air at his imaginary floating embryos. "That's my process."

I waved my own hands to clear away my fart. "Look, I'm presenting a proposal in thirty minutes, and I'm not interested in your process."

"I'm interested," said Danielle.

"We're interested," said the other people on the elevator I'd forgotten about.

Suddenly Starchmont whooped, making us all jump, shaking the elevator, although not hard enough to get us moving again. He began pacing in circles, mumbling something in Urdu about Athena bursting from Zeus's head. After ten circles, I stopped getting out of his way.

"My next play is called . . . um . . ." Starchmont stared at the ceiling for so long, I looked to see if something was written up there.

"*Stuck in an Elevator*," he said finally.

I snorted, hoping everyone else would snort as a show of support, but I got nothing.

"A stuck elevator is a microcosm of humanity," said Starchmont. "It's a pressure cooker for the characters' hopes and dreams—"

"Ouch!" I said, "An idea just came to me. It's called 'A Proposal for the Creation of a Subcommittee to Supervise New Acquisitions.' My proposal burst forth from my head like a flying embryo."

I was ignored. Everyone watched as Starchmont sat on the floor, reached into his beat-up backpack, and pulled out his beat-up laptop.

"Lights up on an elevator in a modern office building," he said as he typed.

Good God, I thought, *he's starting at the beginning.*

"We are introduced to the three major characters," said Starchmont. "A young girl—let's call her Danielle."

Danielle's eyes lit up.

"She longs for a better life, beyond the drudgery of her job in an impersonal office, working with louts who brag about bungee jumps."

Danielle sighed, probably because she could identify with the Danielle character. I waited to see if the bungee jump lout turned out to be the hero.

"There's Grayberg, an artist, an old soul."

"Who sits on the carpet where people track in puke and stuff," I offered.

"And finally," he said, pointing at me. "There's Bong-Cha. A Korean woman."

A pair of Korean women in the elevator clapped.

I gestured toward the Korean women. "Why can't one of the Korean women be the Korean woman?"

"I'm honoring the integrity of my muse," he said in that Urdu language I was getting really sick of.

"A triangle emerges," Starchmont continued. "Danielle is obsessed with Grayberg. Her obsession troubles Bong-Cha, who is deeply in love with Danielle—hm ..."

Starchmont tapped his pursed lips with his forefinger.

"I don't think I can convincingly render a lesbian romance." He pointed at me and declared, "I'm making you Native American."

Surprisingly the Korean women clapped again.

For a moment I almost enjoyed being Native American, until Starchmont told me my name was Weasel Who Crawls on Belly.

I'd had enough. "That'll be a great movie," I said. "Danielle, please move so I can press the alarm button."

Danielle didn't budge.

"My presentation is in ten minutes," I said, barely controlling my rage. "If I don't get out now the Boston cream doughnuts will be gone."

The hatch in the ceiling dropped open, and a balding maintenance man poked his head into the car.

"Everybody okay?" he asked, then, "I get you out. You come up through hatch," he said, dangling an emergency rope ladder.

"Take the ladies first, right after the people who have presentations," I said, reaching for the lowest rung.

"Why you not push button? If you push button I would have come quicker."

"Grayberg is writing a play," said Danielle.

"Really? I write plays."

The maintenance man dropped feetfirst into the car, allowing the rope ladder to fall in a useless heap on the floor.

"I am Stavros Loukanis," he said, pointing to his name tag that read "Nick." "I am rewriting the great Greek tragedies, putting them in modern times."

Danielle and the Korean women smiled at Nick; I stared at the pile of ladder on the floor.

Starchmont continued to type. "The Greek playwright enters from above, like a demigod, and describes his work."

"Instead of king," continued Nick, "Oedipus is now a maintenance man. The theme is universal, speaking to all humanity, but especially to Greek janitors."

At that moment I realized what this play needed: some action. I removed my jacket.

* * *

In the theater, a tableau is a scene where the actors are posed like statues and don't move. When the police and EMS workers pried the elevator doors open, they beheld the tableau of a prone Stavros Loukanis with a bloodied nose, me pinned down by two Korean women, and Danielle with Starchmont's head in her lap, gently rubbing the spot on his head where he'd been repeatedly beaten with his own laptop.

When I got out of jail I visited my old job, even though I was no longer employed there, just to see Danielle. She was at her desk, looking beautiful as ever in spite of bags under her eyes and twenty extra pounds. The temp desk was empty. I put two and two together: Danielle was working longer hours to support both herself and Grayberg Starchmont. She gave me a look that seemed to say, "thanks for beating him in the head, something I feel like doing every night."

I announced to her, "I'm writing a play," as security escorted me out of the building.

Now that I'm home all the time, I sleep until noon and wander around my apartment in my boxers eating saltines—my process. Then I get busy. My play is similar to Grayberg's, only different, called *Waiting for the Elevator Maintenance Man*, kind of like *Waiting for Godot*, only more contemporary because it's set in an elevator. Not sure how my play ends yet. Maybe it ends with me typing these very words. Nah, I don't like it. Back to bed.

THE WALK-IN KING

Lucas Temperley was a loyal young man, and had four hundred letters of recommendation to prove it. He also had two hundred letters acknowledging his resourcefulness, and a couple of Post-it notes praising his good looks.

He got the job.

My dream has come true, he thought, sitting at his temporary desk in the janitorial closet. *Time to start applying myself.*

But before he could apply himself, a distracting thought crept through his brain like a musical earworm: *What did "revenge is a dish best served cold" mean?* He never understood it.

"Never become complacent, Temperley," said Pericles Shinbag, Lucas's boss and CEO of the company.

"I won't, sir."

Shinbag rose from his gigantic desk and walked across his gigantic office to Lucas, who was seated in a tiny, insignificant chair.

"Do you think if I had been complacent, Shinbag Walk-In Enterprises would be what it is today?"

"I don't think that for a moment, sir."

"Sure, I could rest on my laurels if I wanted to. I'm already the biggest supplier of walk-in closets and walk-in bath-and-shower combos on Earth." Shinbag gestured to the framed oil paintings of walk-in closets and walk-in bathtubs adorning his walls.

"I'm the Walk-In King. But I want more, more, more!" Shinbag said, pressing his face close to Lucas. "A company needs to keep growing, like a shark."

He means "like a shark needs to keep moving forward," thought Lucas, biting his tongue.

"Growing like a shark, yes, sir."

"Come up with something else people can walk into. Something else we can corner the market on."

"Yes, sir."

"Think outside the box."

"Yes, sir. I am eager to comply."

* * *

Back at his desk in the janitorial closet, Lucas applied himself to the problem, unaware that his foot was submerged in a bucket of ammonia solution, so hard was he concentrating.

Revenge is a dish best served cold . . .

"Stop it," he scolded his brain. "Focus. Think outside the box . . . "

His single-mindedness was such that he failed to notice Shinbag's daughter, the charming and shapely Prudence Shinbag, as she squeezed into the closet. She had come ostensibly to obtain a can of pest killer, but was in fact seeking to gain Lucas's attention, as she was aroused by his certified good looks.

"Pardon me, I just need the roach spray. I think if I spread my legs and straddle you, I can reach the shelf there behind you."

She did so. Her efforts to obtain insecticide somehow involved rhythmic pelvic thrusts.

"Think outside the box . . ." said Lucas, like a mantra.

After several moments of reaching and thrusting, Prudence stood up.

"There's no multisurface cleaner there," she said.

"I thought you wanted roach spray."

"Oh, right," she said, smoothing the wrinkles in her dress. "I'll come back for that later. Bye, Lucas."

Prudence exited the closet, leaving Lucas to his creative reverie.

"Think outside the box . . . outside the box . . . Ha! I've got it!" he exclaimed, leaping to his feet, splashing ammonia solution on the walls.

"A walk-in box! You start outside the box, then you walk into it!"

* * *

"A walk-in box? Ridiculous!" snorted Pericles Shinbag. "Clearly, hiring you was a mistake. I'm firing you. I also intend to ruin your life."

"Please, Mr. Shinbag . . ."

"Hush. Leave your address with the receptionist as you leave, so we know where to go to ruin you."

After Lucas had trudged out of his boss's office, Shinbag picked up his phone.

"Hello, Research and Development . . . I need to you draw up the schematics for a walk-in box. . . . Well, you walk into it, as opposed to, I don't know, sticking your head in. You figure it out. It's a trillion dollar idea, I tell you . . ."

* * *

Before Lucas could ponder the injustice of being fired, he was given other injustices to ponder.

"Police. Open up."

"How can I help you, officers?" he said to the dozen uniforms at his front door.

"Walk-in box," said the officer in charge. "Good idea."

"Thank you."

"We're arresting you for stealing it from Pericles Shinbag."

"What?! No!"

"I expect you were going to sell the idea to a rival walk-in company."

"There are no rival walk-in companies—"

"Plus I have more trumped-up charges here," said the officer, reading from a list. "Embezzlement, illegal gambling, selling cocaine out of a janitorial closet . . ."

"But . . ." spluttered Lucas, "I didn't do any of those things."

"You probably didn't steal the walk-in box idea either. But Pericles Shinbag is a powerful man. Let's go."

Lucas was handcuffed twelve times, each officer cuffing him so they could all feel they were participating.

* * *

The false charge stuck. Lucas was convicted of first degree idea theft.

Shinbag insisted Lucas be sent to the worst prison in the world, on Dead Man's Rotting Skull with Worms Crawling Out of the Eyeholes Island, in the middle of nowhere. If a prisoner escaped and swam through treacherous shark-infested waters, he would find himself on Stinking Pile of Dung Occupied By Man-Eating Killer Shrews Island, so what was the point?

The prison on Rotting Skull Island held only a single prisoner, and was guarded by a single guard named Lucky Pierre, who was also the warden, the cook, the chaplain, the prison doctor, and sometimes another prisoner who challenged Lucas to a shiv fight, which Pierre would then break up after changing back into his guard uniform.

"Hey, pretty boy!" said Pierre, taunting Lucas through the bars in his tiny cell. "You must have done something really bad to be sent to Rotting Skull Island."

"I was framed."

"I won't be your bitch."

"I don't want you to be my bitch."

"I don't have the wardrobe for it."

"Go away."

Lucas attempted to be alone with his thoughts, not an easy task when Pierre hourly appeared at the door to remind him that he wouldn't be his bitch.

One day, hours passed without interruption, Pierre having swum over to Killer Shrews Island to remind the prisoner there he wouldn't be his bitch.

Finally, some peace, thought Lucas. He drifted into a reverie . . .

Why do I always see animal faces in clouds? . . . Is this thing on the ball of my foot a callus or a wart? . . . If revenge is a dish best served cold, what sort of dish might it be? Certainly not beef stroganoff. . . . It's a little tender so it's probably a wart. . . .

* * *

He snapped awake when the earth on which he was sitting began to move.

What now?

A hole opened up in the dirt and a foul-smelling old man emerged.

"Hello," said the rancid codger. "My name is Maurice LaCroix. I am a prisoner like yourself, from one of the many solitary prison islands in the area."

"I thought there were only two."

"Many more than two. Cavity-Ridden Teeth Sharpened to a Point Island, Entrails from Various Kinds of Cattle Island . . ."

"And you're escaping from—?"

"Egg Salad Left Out in the Sun Too Long Island. Rather than swim to freedom, I thought it might be easier to tunnel out under the sea."

Stupid malodorous old fart, thought Lucas. But he thought it best not to say "malodorous old fart" out loud.

"You've tunneled into another cell, you malodorous old fart—oops, I mean, sir."

"Silly me. I'll be off then. But first, since I'm here, allow me to tutor you in the classical languages."

"All right," acceded Lucas, still feeling guilty about the "old fart" remark.

Lucas applied himself to the study of Latin, Greek, Chinese, and Arabic. He knew one of the fastest ways to learn was to teach, so he taught Lucky Pierre to say "I won't be your bitch" in Sanskrit.

LaCroix, with a growing affection for the young prisoner, broadened his studies to include needlepoint, self-shiatsu massage, the history of the cups-and-balls illusion, Welsh clog dancing, and other essential life skills.

But as Lucas's abilities grew, so did his resentment of this invasion of privacy. One day, while practicing a toby step as he recited the Song of Ilium, he could no longer contain himself.

"Crawl back in your hole!" he blurted.

Loyal, faithful, and true Lucas Temperley surprised himself, and surprised LaCroix too.

"Lucas, you've changed."

"No, I don't think I have," said Lucas, then contradicted himself by shoving the gamy old man headfirst down the hole he had dug, covering it up, and tamping down the sod.

Lucas had learned much from Maurice LaCroix. But in the end, the most valuable lesson he learned was how to deal with people harshly. This was the new Lucas Temperley: a talented needlepoint artist, obsessed with vengeance.

Revenge on Pericles Shinbag.

Lucas still didn't know what sort of dish revenge was, but he was determined to serve it, or eat it, or something.

First, though, he would have to escape. In this endeavor, fortune favored him. The authorities needed his cell for another unjustly convicted victim, so he was evicted. After saying goodbye to a tearful Lucky Pierre, who admitted he had wanted to be his bitch all along, Lucas took a dinghy to the mainland.

* * *

Meanwhile, Pericles Shinbag had triumphed with the walk-in box, thanks to an aggressive marketing campaign aimed at senior citizens who feared they could never again climb into a box without assistance.

Out of prison, Lucas created a new identity for himself, inspired by old man LaCroix's Arabic-language instruction: he became the Arab prince, Adi al-Temperley. He disguised himself with a turban and Groucho glasses, thinking, *I can wear the glasses, fake nose, and moustache. Or the glasses and nose. Or the glasses alone. In this way, I can be several different Arab princes, if the need arises.*

After winning an international Welsh clog dancing competition, and then making a fortune in commercial endorsements for Nike clogging shoes, he was ready.

First, Lucas would manipulate the people in Shinbag's life, as a sort of warm-up.

He paid Shinbag's dry cleaner and Shinbag's dentist to trade places. Thus, Shinbag endured hours of agony in the dentist chair, and his shirts were returned with marinara stains on the front.

He trained Shinbag's German shepherd Rolf to bite Shinbag in the shins whenever Shinbag said, "Stop biting me, Rolf."

And then Lucas appeared to Prudence Shinbag in disguise as Sheik Adi al-Temperley. He told her that Lucas (whom he knew intimately) had drowned in shark-infested waters during an escape attempt. As he was going under, he wrote a note on a passing grouper: "At least this way I'll never have to marry that pushy Prudence Shinbag." The news caused her to kill herself; after that she sought refuge in a convent for dead nuns.

* * *

"Sorry about your daughter."

Shinbag shrugged. "Perhaps with the dead nuns, she'll find the peace that eluded her in life. Why have you brought me here?"

"My idea will make us both wealthy men," said Sheik al-Temperley, reclining comfortably on plush cushions in the back of his deluxe minivan.

Pericles Shinbag shifted uncomfortably and rubbed his jaw, the dry cleaner's root canal still tormenting him.

"I'm already a wealthy man, Sheik."

Lucas leaned forward conspiratorially. He began to remove his Groucho glasses for emphasis, then stopped himself in time.

"Wealthy enough to afford a luxurious minivan like this?" Sheik al-Temperley gestured to the tapestries on the wall; he inhaled deeply of the intoxicating vapors provided by censers suspended from the ceiling.

Shinbag got a faraway money-grubbing look in his eyes. He had limos. Of course he had limos. Every billionaire had limos. But a minivan? His billionaire friends would turn green with envy.

"Tell me more."

"I provide the idea, you provide the manufacturing and distribution. We split the profits fifty-fifty."

"Forty for you." Shinbag pointed to the Sheik. "Seventy for me," he said, touching his chest.

"You drive a hard, ludicrous bargain. Very well."

"And," said Shinbag, "we name the product after me. I am after all the Walk-In King."

"So be it," nodded Lucas. "We'll call it the Shinbag Walk-In Brick Wall. I'll show you the schematics."

Shinbag immediately began choosing colors for the unicorn he wanted airbrushed on the side of his Kia Sedona. He rushed the Walk-In Brick Wall into production almost as an afterthought.

The results were immediately catastrophic.

Millions of loyal Shinbag customers, who for years had enjoyed walking into his bathtubs, closets, and boxes, now found themselves with concussed foreheads and chipped incisors. Medical bills totaled in the trillions.

His mysterious Arab partner had vanished. The lawsuits bankrupted Shinbag many times over.

"What do you want?" croaked an emaciated Shinbag through the bars of his tiny cell.

"I won't be your bitch," said Lucky Pierre, licking his lips. "You'll be *my* bitch."

* * *

Lucas Temperley sat cross-legged atop his minivan, parked on a seaside cliff. His Groucho glasses lay on his lap, no longer required, having served him well.

He gazed out across the ocean and smiled, thinking, *Somewhere out there, something very unpleasant is being done to Pericles Shinbag.*

And then Lucas understood.

"*Revenge is a dish best served cold.*" Don't take revenge in the heat of the moment. Wait until it has cooled, meaning "wait a while."

Well, that's nonsense, thought Lucas. *If I'd waited I wouldn't be where I am now. There must be a better metaphor.*

"*Revenge is a walk-in bathtub. You walk in and then . . .*"

He couldn't finish the thought. His elaborate revenge scheme had consumed every erg of his mental energy. His brilliant mind could no longer generate a metaphor.

This was the man Lucas Temperley had become.

THE HITMAN CONVENTION

The old man with thick glasses seemed incapable of understanding my key chains.

It was to be expected, I suppose. The key chains, tiny rowboats that read THE GARDENER on the side, probably sent a mixed message.

"Young fella, you're telling me you have nothing to do with boats?" he said.

"No."

"You're in the gardening business?"

"Not exactly."

The gardening business? What a stupid question. If I were a real gardener, why would I be at the hitman trade show?

Resisting the urge to snap at the old codger, because everyone is a potential customer, I explained how when you hire the Gardener—me—for a hit, you get not just a killing but a flower garden too, both for the same low price.

Behind the heavy lenses, his gaze drifted around the convention center. I didn't want to lose him. He was the only person who'd stopped at my booth all morning.

Putting my arm around his bony shoulders, I elaborated. "My method is aesthetically beautiful. Your chosen victim is led to a remote spot in the woods where the soil is loose and easy to turn over. I provide him with a shovel. I know, I know, plenty of hitmen force their victims to dig their own graves. Those guys over there, for example."

I gestured to the rows of booths, dozens of them, occupied by traditional hitmen, wearing the same old dark suits and the same old name tags reading HI, MY NAME IS VINCE, offering to kill your victim the same old way and dump them in the same old forest preserve.

"They're all the same," he observed.

"Exactly. Here's what sets me apart: I force the victim to plant flowers around his grave."

"Why?"

"Because I'm the Gardener! Sorry, didn't mean to shout."

"Then why the boats?" he said, picking up a key chain.

I should have expected this. I explained how I had wanted key chains shaped like trowels, but they'd all been sold to a hitman called the Bricklayer. Competition at the trade show was stiff.

"So how about it?" I said, putting on a little pressure. "Who would you like bumped off?"

"I don't know. Maybe someday you can kill my wife," he said, trying to be nice, as he wriggled away from my arm.

I let him go.

"My number's on the boat."

"I used to own a dinghy," he said, as he helped himself to several more key chains and hurried away.

He must've got his dates wrong. The boat show wouldn't be here for another week, when the International Hitman Trade Show ended. Chicago's McCormick Place was booked solid.

I saw no need to worry about my slow morning. My business concept was as strong as the other concept hitmen around me. They were thriving. I knew my time would come.

From where I stood I could see a crowd lining up to talk to the Travel Agent. He disposed of his bodies by buying them a first-class ticket, buckling their seat belt over their blanket, then asking the flight attendant to just let them sleep.

Next to him was the Cannibal, hugely overweight, so I guess business was good for him too.

Further along was the Taxidermist who would shoot his victims and walk away. I suggested he was missing a bet by not stuffing the corpses, but he said that idea was taken by the Mummifier. Like I said, competition was stiff.

Most popular of all was the Rocketeer, who crammed his dead victims into a missile and planned to shoot it into space. It was a sexy idea, but because of the high cost of liquid nitrogen, he needed another seven hundred bodies to break even.

These were my people, the novelty hitmen, original and creative. They were supportive, unlike the old-school Vince killers, who wouldn't give me the time of day.

"Don't be discouraged, pal. It takes time to build a business," said the Cannibal, passing by my booth. He burped and picked his teeth with his pinky fingernail, having just delivered on a contract.

Other than my own, the only other booth that wasn't mobbed was the one next to me. It belonged to a young brunette with sad eyes. I saw she was offering key chains shaped like scissors that read THE STYLIST.

"Hello, Stylist. I'm the Gardener. Calvin Blister."

"Joyce Harms."

"How does that work, being the Stylist? You do your victim's hair before or after you kill them?"

"After."

"Isn't that messy?"

"Okay, before."

For a moment we watched people passing our booths and approaching the Rocketeer, well on his way to his seven hundred bodies.

"You've never actually killed anyone, have you?" I said to Joyce.

Joyce shrugged. "I've styled a lot of people."

"Ah. I've done a lot of gardening."

"How about you? Ever kill anybody?"

I shook my head. We had something in common. I was thinking I'd like to know this hitperson better.

"Want to get some coffee?" she said, reading my mind.

"Excuse me," said a tiny old woman. "Could you please plant some begonias?"

I looked down at her. "Sure. After I kill someone."

"Oh dear."

"I won't be gone long. Think about who you want me to kill," I said, then followed Joyce to the convention center exit.

"Oh dear."

* * *

We strolled along the lakefront, sipping our lattes. Turns out Joyce thought a life of crime held a romantic appeal, just like me. And like me, she had an enormous student loan to pay off.

"Calvin, when you finally kill somebody, how will you do it?"

"I'm thinking it would be great if I could club them to death with tulip bulbs. That way I'd have fewer things to carry."

"Well," said Joyce, taking a pair of shears out of her purse, "I should probably kill my victim with the same shears I use to do their hair, don't you think? Maybe slit their throat?"

She made a sudden throat-slashing motion across my neck. The shears missed me by half an inch.

"Whoa!" I said, snapping my head back. "Yeah, that would work."

"Just give them a fast cut." She sliced through the air again, coming even closer to my Adam's apple.

"Please put the scissors away."

She dropped her latte on the ground and held her weapon with both hands.

"Or maybe a stabbing motion." She raised the shears above her head.

I'd been on dates that went from casual conversation to attempted murder, but never this quickly.

Dancing from side to side to avoid her thrusts, I blurted, "Why are you doing this?"

"I like you."

"I like you too."

"Please, I need to establish my street cred."

Her scissors caught my sleeve and ripped it open.

I ran.

She pursued me along the lakefront and back to the convention center. I threw open the doors, running inside as she gave chase, shears held high.

We both froze.

Seated in her booth was a guy in a black suit named Vince.

"I'm the Stylist," said Vince.

"No you're not," said Joyce.

"Yeah, I am. And him over there," he said, jerking his thumb, "he's the Gardener."

The Vince in my booth gave me an unfriendly wave.

With growing horror, Joyce and I surveyed our corner of the convention center. Gone were the Cannibal, the Taxidermist, the Travel Agent, and the Rocketeer, their booths now occupied by identical Vinces.

"They got rid of our friends. Let's take them down," she said, advancing with her scissors.

"Wait." I gently held her back. "Maybe they went to lunch."

I approached the Rocketeer's booth.

"Where did our friends go?"

Rocketeer Vince smiled, showing several gold teeth. "They took a trip to the forest preserve."

Vinces within earshot laughed coarsely, revealing a blinding array of shining yellow dental work.

I returned to Joyce, still holding her shears high.

"They're not at lunch," I said. "My guess is, they killed our friends for taking away their business."

"Look at that asshole, pocketing my key chains."

"Joyce, no."

She slipped past me, sneaking up behind Vince the Stylist.

Unfortunately she hadn't oiled her scissors. The hinge was rusty.

Squeak.

Vince the Stylist spun around. He opened his mouth and emitted a high-pitched sound that only Vinces could hear.

Every black suit in McCormick Place snapped to attention. They slipped their hands inside their jackets and felt for their weapons, ready to come to the aid of their endangered associate.

"Joyce, run!"

I grabbed her free hand and together we dashed for the doors, weaving and scrambling like Heisman Trophy winners, finally bursting outside as four hundred hitmen tried to crunch through the front exit and fell in a tangled heap.

We stopped on the sidewalk for a moment to catch our breath.

"I'm sorry I lost it back there," said Joyce.

"Death is in the air. It's understandable. Hey, there's a cop."

I ran up to the redheaded uniformed officer, currently writing a parking ticket for a black sedan in a handicapped space.

"Excuse me, Officer."

"This sort of thing really pisses me off."

"Are you aware of what's happening inside?"

"Can't be as bad as bad as what's happening out here. What if my grandmother wanted this space?"

"There are dozens of hired killers inside."

"She's ninety-two and still drives—. Wait, what did you say?"

"Isn't it illegal to commit murder for hire?"

"You're darn right it is. That's the first thing they teach us at the academy."

At once the convention center doors burst open, ejecting a flood of gorillas.

The young officer held up his hand.

"Hold it right there."

The Vinces halted. It must have been the uniform.

"Any of you guys hitmen?"

They lowered their heads and shifted their weight from side to side, mumbling, "No, sir."

Joyce and I crept away.

* * *

We gave up the idea of becoming killers, having learned it was even more dangerous than being victims.

We still had student loans to pay off. So Joyce became a real stylist. She nearly stabbed her first customer to death, but at the last second came to her senses and applied conditioner instead.

I began planting flowers in shallow graves instead of people. Yeah, now I'm a real gardener.

After a public outcry, the city weighed the loss of life against the loss of revenue, and outlawed the hitman convention. But that didn't stop the Vinces, who went underground, trading their black suits for white aprons, then renting booths at the Housewares Convention.

The password was "nonstick cookware."

MEET YOUR ENLIGHTENED SELF

It's hard to imagine how a weekly book club meeting could leave a person feeling empty inside. But it did. And that person was me.

Our meeting was winding down, and it had been a good one, or at least Diane and Jocelyn thought so. They had gotten into an in-depth discussion over *Clean Your Closet, Clean Your Brain!* It was an awesome and outstanding book, but I just sort of sat there, and after twenty minutes they'd run out of things to say about it. As they were putting on their coats, and I was clearing the wine tumblers and the snack plates, I said:

"Hey guys. I have a suggestion for next week's book."

"Is it *My Closet Is My Palace?*" said Diane. "I'm dying to read that in paperback."

"No," I said. "That looks like a fun one, and I'm dying to read it too. But I was thinking of this."

I reached under the sofa cushions and produced my dog-eared copy of *Let Your Enlightened Self Be Your Guide.*

"Hm," said Diane.

"Your guide to what?" said Jocelyn. "Decluttering your sock drawer?"

"No," I said. "Or if it is, I haven't gotten to that part yet. But it's still really good."

I explained to them how I had searched for a short spiritual book. This one ran less than one hundred pages, a sweet spot for us.

The gist of it was, what if your future enlightened self traveled back in time to the present day, and gave you smart advice?

"If it's not about your sock drawer, what is your future self enlightened about?" said Jocelyn.

"I don't know. Just enlightened." I found a dog-eared page and read ". . . your self who has achieved *satori*. That's Hindu-ese for 'enlightened.'"

"Suh-tore-ee," repeated Diane.

"Like the Japanese beer," said Jocelyn.

"Kinda," I said.

"Well, okee-doke, Annie," said Diane. "We'll read it, if you think we should. You make the best snacks."

"Yum," said Jocelyn.

The guys left. I sat on the sofa and read another page of *Let Your Enlightened Self Be Your Guide*, more excited about a book than I'd been in a long time. I imagined meeting my future enlightened self, Annie (because that's her name, because she's me). I tried to think of a spiritual question to ask her, but all I came up with was "How long should I keep sweaters I haven't worn in two years?" Not really a spiritual question, I suppose. Just what was on my mind after the closet-book discussion.

I shared my excitement about the spiritual book with my husband, Larry.

"That's good," said Larry.

"What questions would you ask *your* future self?" I said.

"That's good," said Larry.

Larry had a knack for hiding his excitement.

* * *

The next morning, I kissed Larry at the front door before he headed off to work.

"What would you like for dinner?" I asked him.

"That's good," he said, walking away.

An hour later, the doorbell rang.

I opened the door. A bald man stood there, with droopy eyes and a droopy mouth, wearing a wrinkled jacket and a wrinkled tie. Wrinkled and bald and droopy. The words "sad sack" came to mind.

"Hello," I said. "Can I help you?"

"I am your enlightened future self."

I said nothing. For a long time. Then I said:

"No, you're not."

"From the future."

"You're a man."

"From the distant future," he clarified.

"It's too early to be joking."

"I didn't get your name," he said.

"I didn't give it."

He just stood there. He may have thought there was something compelling about his sad-sackiness. If he did, he was wrong.

"Okay, I'm Annie," I said.

"Hello, Annie. Obviously, my name is also Annie. I'm your enlightened— "

I slammed the door.

Sad Sack rang the bell again.

"Don't you want advice from your enlightened self? I feel it's my duty to give you counsel," he said, planting his foot in the doorway like an old timey door-to-door salesman.

"Don't want your counsel, thank you very much."

"Ow. Ow. Ow," said Sad Sack, as I repeatedly banged the door on his foot.

"Just let me—ow—let me give you one piece of advice. Two pieces, actually. Then I'll go, I promise."

"What?"

"Keep an open mind about how your future enlightened self could be a man."

"Okay, no. What's the second piece?"

He took a deep breath, then said, "The trouble is, you think you have time. You don't. So cherish every precious second."

I stopped crushing his foot.

I said *wow* to myself. I thought about how I mostly go along on autopilot. Like a machine. Then I wonder why, at the end of the day, I feel empty inside.

"That's pretty good advice," I said.

"Right? Can I have a glass of water?"

"Um . . . sure. Wait here."

I got a glass of water for Annie Sad Sack. He downed it in one gulp, dribbling half of it down his stained shirt.

"Thanks."

He gave me back the glass, then turned and limped away.

Later, when Larry came home, I said, "A strange man came by this morning . . ."

"That's good."

"Wait, let me finish. He claimed to be my enlightened self from the future. I smashed his foot in the doorway. He gave me advice about cherishing every moment. Then he drank a glass of water."

"That's good," Larry elaborated.

I cherished Larry's response.

* * *

My doorbell rang the next morning.

"Who is it?" I called out.

"Annie from the future."

I opened the door. He was using a broken mop handle for a cane, as if he needed to look even sadder.

"I've been cherishing moments," I blurted.

"That's good," he said, sounding a lot like Larry.

"I still don't believe you're my enlightened self from the future. But since I saw you yesterday I've cherished seven moments."

"And how do you feel?"

"Good. A tiny bit more enlightened."

"I'm glad to hear it."

I smiled.

"Can we order a pizza?" he said.

* * *

When he said order *a* pizza, what he really meant was *three* pizzas.

He rested comfortably in our living room, his damaged foot elevated on an ottoman. As he shoveled slices of Pizza Number Three into his mouth, pepperoni slices fell on the front of his jacket and looked like giant red buttons on a clown suit.

"Practice mindfulness," he said with his mouth full.

"Is that like cherishing every moment?"

"Kind of. Mindfulness is being aware of what you're doing all the time."

"Like cherishing?"

He nodded. "Cherishing, washing dishes, brushing your teeth. Everything."

"Okay, I'll try it, Mister . . ."

"Annie. Call me Annie."

"I'm not comfortable calling you Annie. Is there a different name I can use?"

He removed a mushroom trapped in his front teeth and thought for a moment.

"I've always liked the name Constantine."

"I'm going to call you Stu," I said, thinking that was a better name for a sad sack than Constantine.

"So, Stu . . . ," I said, as he made a face. "How do I start being mindful?"

"Why not mindfully pick up your phone and order some fried chicken?"

* * *

We spent the first half hour of our weekly book club meeting discussing the most attractive finish for wall-mounted closet hooks, with Diane arguing passionately for cast iron, Jocelyn swearing she would lay down her life for antique brass, and me knowing in my heart it was imitation walnut or nothing.

And all the time I'm thinking, *As interesting as this discussion is, I'd rather be cherishing moments of mindfulness.*

"Did you guys read the book about your future enlightened self?"

I must confess, my jaw dropped open when they both nodded.

"So good," said Diane.

"So good," said Jocelyn.

"Loved the cherishing," said Diane.

"Loved the mindfulness," said Jocelyn.

"You guys, that's so great! Although I must tell you, it's kind of weird. My enlightened self is a man."

They shook their heads.

"Not weird at all," said Diane.

"Keep an open mind," said Jocelyn.

"I don't like calling my enlightened self Annie," I explained, "so I call him Stu."

"I call my enlightened self Constantine, 'cause he likes that," said Diane.

"That's funny," said Jocelyn. "My enlightened self likes Constantine too."

Okay. I was beginning to get the picture.

"Are we talking about a sad-looking bald man?"

"Yes," they said in unison.

"Wrinkled suit with pepperoni clown buttons?"

"Yes! Yes! Yes!"

"It's the same guy, and he's pulling a fast one."

"Keep an open mind," whimpered Jocelyn.

I clenched my fists. "He's been using me to get delivery food!"

"He's been using me for clothes," said Diane. "Not only did I buy him a new suit, but I ironed wrinkles into it for him, too!"

"He's staying at our house!" said Jocelyn.

"In your spare bedroom?"

"No, in our entire house. We're sleeping in the garage."

I thought, *We've acted stupidly, with Jocelyn acting more stupidly than Diane and me*, but that thought gave me little comfort.

"You know what?" said Jocelyn, sounding intelligent for a change. "He's just some guy who listened at the window, heard you talk about the enlightened self book, and now he's taking advantage."

"He's a voyeur," said Diane.

"Not only that, but he was spying on us," said Jocelyn. I guess her moment of intelligence had passed.

"Let's make him pay," said Diane, cracking knuckles I didn't know she had.

"One second," I said. "Let's not be hasty. He did give us valuable advice. Did he tell you to cherish each moment?"

"Yes," they said.

"And did he tell you to be mindful?"

"Yes."

"So maybe the good advice makes up for the times he took advantage."

"Then what do you think we should do?" said Diane.

By default, I was the leader, since I served the best snacks. They looked to me, waiting for instructions.

"Let's kill him."

* * *

It's a good thing Jocelyn was acquainted with the hiding places in her own home. We found him huddled in a closet under the staircase.

Three angry women versus one slow-moving, pizza-engorged sad sack. Not good odds for Constantine/Stu.

"Cherish each moment—UGH!"

I rammed my fist into his midsection.

"Practice mindfulness—OW!"

Diane caught him under the jaw with a left hook.

"Win the day—GREAT GOD IN HEAVEN!"

Jocelyn slammed him to the floor with a double-leg flapjack.

"Saw that on the WWE last week," she said as we clapped her on the back.

He didn't get up. He lay there, moaning.

"Think he's had enough?" said Diane.

We knew the answer to that—he hadn't. We pulled him to his feet and prepared to give him another round.

His eyes spun around like slot machine reels. Somehow, he recovered and focused on me. As I prepared to pummel his torso again, he said:

"A step stool makes it easier to reach the upper shelves of your clothes closet."

I hesitated, my fist poised in midair.

Could it be? Dare I think that now, finally, I could know what items had been shoved to the back of the topmost recesses of my walk-in? I could tell by the glazed look in my friends' eyes that they were awed by the same possibility.

"An over-the-door shoe rack can be used," said Stu, "not only for shoes, but for other accessories as well."

We trembled. A tearful Jocelyn fell to her knees. "Forgive me for the power drop."

Stu placed a benevolent hand on her head, comforting her.

"Annie," he said, "I was hungry and you fed me. Diane, even though I wasn't naked, you clothed me. Jocelyn, thanks for your house."

He closed his eyes. Shafts of brilliant light came pouring down on him from the heavens. He spoke once more.

"By hanging colored divider tags on cardstock, you can easily sort through different types of clothing, so you can find exactly what you're searching for."

Maybe he had overheard us talking about closets. Who knows? Who cares? I pushed that thought to the back of my mind.

"Truly," I declared to the others, "this man is our enlightened selves from the future."

* * *

"That's good," said Larry.

"I didn't say anything," I told him.

"That's good."

MR. DUNK TANK

"Bozo is dying."

I tried to imagine I was a small child, crying when I heard the news. But I didn't cry. Because this wasn't the Bozo children love. This was Bozo, my father, the dunk tank clown.

Actually, I did cry a little, because I hated my father and I'd have to take time off from work. And I hated him. Did I mention that?

My name is Wallace "Don't Call Me Wally" Petrie, and I'm a highly paid idea man. You may have heard of my company: Idea Men, Inc. I am the only employee, having had the idea to fire all the other idea men.

I should explain what a dunk-tank clown does. You find him at a traveling carnival, sitting on a plank over a tank of rancid water, wearing clown makeup that looks like he applied it with a dead squirrel's tail. He needs makeup so no one recognizes him later, because his job is to scream insults at people on the carnival midway, hoping they'll pay hard-earned money to hurl baseballs at a target that will release the plank and drop him into the mucky drink. My father took pride in his work, and now I had to drop everything so I could be with this clown on his death bed.

* * *

I guess I did owe him something. He raised me as a single parent in the carnival. My mother was a frustrated lesbian who ran away with a bearded man, thinking it was a bearded lady. My father wanted me to

217

follow in his soggy footsteps and become a Bozo. When I was a baby, he'd teach me insults to hurl at the crowd, and my first words were "When you got your hair cut, did they let you keep the bowl?" Then at bath time he'd place me on the plank and throw balls until I'd been dunked clean. He set up a college fund for me, which soon became his bourbon fund.

These memories haunted me as I left the city and hit the open highway. The only address I had for my father was:

BOZO

THE DUNK TANK

C/O THE CARNIVAL

USA

* * *

I found him in southern Illinois.

It was early afternoon, a few hours before the carnival opened. I was met by Bev, the young woman who worked the front of the tank, charging people ten dollars for twelve baseballs to throw at the target.

"Your father is very ill, but he still insists on working," said Bev, counting the bills in her canvas apron. Sure enough, there was my dad in a hospital bed, balanced on the plank.

"What does he have?" I asked.

"I can't remember the medical name," said Bev, "but it's commonly known as dunk-tank lung."

"Occupational hazard, I suppose."

"There are misconceptions about the disease. You don't have to be a dunk-tank clown to get dunk-tank lung."

"Surprising."

"You can get it from hanging around a dunk-tank clown. I'm fine, I've had my shots."

"Wally?" said my father hoarsely. "Is that you? Come closer."

He looked very much the same. Scraggly hair. Frayed bib overalls. Clown white smeared on his face.

"You made it, Wally."

"It's Wallace."

"It should be Bozo."

He was seized with a sudden fit of coughing.

"Are you getting treatment?"

"There's a clinic that specializes in dunk-tank lung."

"Then that's where you should be."

"My luck's been bad. It's a traveling clinic, like a carnival, and we've never been in the same town at the same time."

Another coughing fit, followed by a jolt that almost dropped his bed into the water.

"Hey!" I shouted at a couple kids who had sneaked in early. "Stop throwing baseballs. Can't you see he's dying?"

"This tank, the cage, the Bozo banner, the baseballs—I own it all. It's my estate. Some clowns go their whole lives renting a tank. Not me."

"Yeah, that's great, Dad. Look, I can't promise I'll keep the tank when you die. I don't have much use for it in the city."

"Come closer," he said. I poked my head through the bars.

"You're not getting my tank. I'm leaving it to Bev."

"The girl with the baseballs?"

"Yeah. You don't deserve it."

"Hold on," I said, beginning to get angry in spite of myself. "Actually, I *do* deserve it because I'm your son."

"You're not. A *real* son would sit on a plank like it was his throne. He would hurl insults at the midway, beholden to no man."

"Until he got wet."

"You're not good enough to be a dunk-tank clown."

"I own my own consulting firm. I take home six figures a year."

"You're a pansy. You could never do what I do."

"Why would I even want to?"

"You're an ack ack."

"Dad?"

Ack ack weren't words. He was finished.

* * *

Bozos came from across the country for the funeral. Because my father owned his tank, he was a figure of great respect. In his honor, the clowns gave Dad one final dunk. They placed his body on a plank over an open grave, then threw fistfuls of dirt at the target. I cried; I admit it.

* * *

"I don't want the damn tank," said Bev.

"But he left it to you in his will."

"I want nothing more to do with the dunk tank. Finally, I'm free to pursue my dream."

"What's that?"

"Working the beanbag toss."

"If you're gonna dream, dream big."

* * *

The carny owner told me to get my father's tank the hell off the midway. With no clown in it, the tank was just taking up space that could be used for rigged games of chance.

I loaded the tank and everything else into a big trailer and drove off in my father's truck. I thought I'd try to sell the tank on eBay, along with an autographed photo of Adam Sandler I didn't want anymore. But then I got to thinking: Maybe I'd keep the tank. Maybe I could make a few bucks, doing what my father did in his crappy chosen career.

* * *

My first idea was to abandon the old convention of the dunk-tank clown insulting people. It was the twenty-first century. They had dunk tanks at schools and church functions, for crying out loud. Surely a considerate clown could be more effective than an abusive one.

I found a new carnival and gave the dunk-tank clown, Chuckles, five hundred dollars to change his name to Chuckles the Emotionally Supportive Clown. Then I hired a girl, Polly, to handle the baseballs. She'd been giving darts to people to throw at balloons but wanted to add dunk-tank girl to her resume.

From my hiding place next to the tank, I coached Chuckles on the new lines I wanted him to shout down the midway:

"You're not fat, you're fine just the way you are."

"You can achieve anything you put your mind to."

"Let your smile change the world."

Chuckles spent more time in the tank than he did on the plank. The line was a quarter mile long, of people wanting to dunk him with his endless stream of positive messages. I'd really hit on something.

I bought dozens of tanks. I ran workshops that taught clowns to help people see the best in themselves, and people really hated it. The business exploded.

* * *

I had hundreds of employees. My dunk-tank empire was making history. It earned the me the title Mr. Dunk Tank. But an idea man can't simply turn off the idea faucet.

What if instead of water, the tank was filled with amaretto, and after you dunked the clown, you got to lick it off his body? (Okay, sometimes you had to throw off some bad ideas to get to the gold.)

What if the tank was on an airplane, and when you hit the target, the clown would fall out the bottom and plummet to the ground? This was popular with the Bozos who were worried about contracting dunk-tank lung and wanted to die some other way.

What if dunking one clown wasn't enough? What if you could dunk an entire production of *Waiting for Godot*? People paid a hundred dollars per baseball to do just that, and they loved it, especially if it meant not having to sit through the entire play.

These last two ideas were smashing successes. I was riding high. High and dry, as they say in the dunk-tank business.

Soon, Hollywood celebrities were dying to get in on the action. Stars fell over themselves to throw parties and get dunked, and they paid top dollar to have their swimming pools reduced to dunk-tank size. Swimming pool reduction companies thrived. I had a piece of that, in addition to owning stock in the Hollywood plank industry.

I had to hand it to my father. His reverse psychology worked on me. Was he smart enough to know about reverse psychology? I don't think he was. I think he was just a stupid old dunk-tank clown.

Then everything came crashing down, into the tank, metaphorically.

* * *

I was working in my Los Angeles office, in the penthouse of Mr. Dunk Tank corporate headquarters. (Address: One Dunk-Tank Plaza.) I was working on an idea for a zero-gravity dunk tank where, when you hit the target, the clown would float up and away into outer space. I wanted to have it ready for when intergalactic travel to intergalactic carnivals became affordable.

I glanced out the window. On the street fifty floors below, a small car pulled up and lawyers began piling out, one after another. I counted a thousand. What was even more amazing was the figure who followed the lawyers out of the car:

Bev, my dad's old baseball holder.

"These are my attorneys," said Bev. She and the others had crowded into my office.

"I like it better when clowns come out of a clown car," I said.

The attorneys growled as one.

"They don't like it when you call it a clown car," said Bev.

"Where does a dunk-tank ball girl get the money for all these lawyers?"

"I'm not a dunk-tank ball girl anymore," she said, even though she still wore her canvas apron, now bulging with thousand-dollar bills.

"Your father left me his dunk tank. Technically I'm still the owner. And since that tank is the foundation of your empire, I am legally entitled to everything you own."

I realized with a sinking feeling I didn't stand a chance in a court of law, not against a thousand attorneys.

"I'm the new Mr. Dunk Tank," she said. A thousand lawyers presented me with documents declaring she was now legally Mr. Dunk Tank. It took a few hours.

"Now get out," said Bev.

Just like that.

Under the hostile eyes of Bev and her attorneys, I walked to the door, taking nothing but the clothes on my back.

"I hope you all die of dunk tank lung!" I shouted, then exited before they could catch me.

* * *

"Here's an idea: go fornicate yourself!" I shouted at the redneck with the shaved head.

Polly gave him three baseballs. He dropped me in the water with his first throw.

Splash.

As I came up spluttering and climbed back on my plank, I shouted, "Here's an even better idea—go fornicate yourself twice!"

Splash.

Life was good. I had Polly. I had my own tank.

I wasn't Wally. I wasn't Bozo. I was different. I was better. I was Idea Man the Clown.

Take that, Dad.

THERE ARE NIGHTMARES, AND THEN THERE'S THIS

I am running through the forest. I think that's what I'm doing. I'm placing one foot in front of the other. Do I have enough feet? I assume so, but I'm too busy running to count them. I'm breathing heavy, passing through trees and underbrush, and if that's not running through the forest, you tell me what is.

I might be running away from something, so I glance over my shoulder.

I fall, tripping on a root and landing face down in leaves. Leaves on my face. Cool and damp. It is a relief. Re-leaf. Ha ha.

My relief doesn't last long.

I hear running feet. I know the sound, from personal experience.

I turn my head.

I see four tiny feet, like on a squirrel. My eyes travel up from the feet to the face, not a long trip. I see puffy cheeks. I see a bushy tail.

Yep. Squirrel.

It comes close to my face and sniffs.

Then it speaks! "Hello."

I do not respond.

"Hello," chirps the squirrel.

Every fiber of my being is screaming, screaming in terror and rage at this abomination of nature, this bushy-tailed atrocity. But my scream is a silent scream, an inner scream that deafens my inner ear.

As if its grotesque greeting is not enough, the squirrel continues. "Are you okay?"

It's nightmarish. It occurs to me, this may be a nightmare.

My pulse quickens. Frozen with dread, I cannot move. And yet I know I must. With supreme effort I draw my feet underneath my body and rise.

I discover I am now taller than the squirrel. But my physical superiority does little to calm my terror.

The squirrel is not done with me. It looks up and squeaks, "Want a nut?"

I run, laughing insanely in an attempt to stay sane, laughing madly at the madness of a world gone mad.

Running away from the squirrel. Running to safety. Running to sanity.

Or so I think.

Crashing through underbrush. Crashing into a clearing.

A bear is there.

"Howdy," it says, its voice a lazy rumble.

I freeze. I do not respond. If I wouldn't talk to a squirrel, why would I talk to a bear?

"Pretty day, ain't it?" it continues.

And then, in a flash, I know what I must do.

I must wake myself from this nightmare.

"Wake up"—as I slap my face. "Wake up"—as I tug the hair on my forearm.

"That's gotta hurt," says the bear.

Seven other bears emerge from the underbrush and join the first bear, forming a conga line and slapping each other's bottoms in a rumba rhythm.

"Wake up"—as I stomp on my toes.

The bears sing: "THAT'S GOTTA HURT. THAT'S GOTTA HURT . . ."

"Wake up"—as I poke twigs up my nose.

"OUCH OUCH OUCH OUCH . . . ," sing the bears as they slowly advance on me.

"Wake up!" I scream.

I am not waking up.

I run.

And then, suddenly, I am lying in a field of flowers.

The flowers have faces. Pretty lady faces, with big eyes and long lashes, and full pouty lady lips. Some of the flowers wear makeup, which strikes me as unnecessary.

The flowers sing, in four-part harmony:

"COME WITH US DOWN TO THE WATER. COME WITH US DOWN TO THE WATER . . ."

I'm getting used to this sort of thing, which makes it no less bone-chilling.

In lieu of waking up, which I can't seem to manage, I decide to follow the flowers down to the water.

There is an uncomfortable moment where the flowers sing:

"COME WITH US DOWN TO THE WATER..."

But they don't move, and I realize they're planted in the ground. They *can't* move. They sing, "COME WITH US," more impatiently now, as if to say, "It's a figurative invitation, dummy, just move." This makes the moment socially awkward, in addition to nightmarish.

The flowers part, leaning aside really, making a path. They gesture with their heads, indicating I should follow the path, which I do eagerly to avoid further embarrassment.

And now I see the squirrel again. It offers me a nut as I pass. I politely decline, thinking, *You'll get rid of more nuts if you're less pushy.*

The bears arrive too, slapping each other's bottoms with one forepaw and pointing the way with the other.

And then I'm at the water.

I see the glassy pond quietly reflecting the white clouds and blue sky above.

The squirrel and the bears and the flowers hold their collective breath.

I lean forward and look at my reflection.

My skin is smooth and pale. My hair is dark brown, parted on the side. My teeth are white and even. I have a neatly groomed mustache. I wear stylish, wire-rimmed glasses.

I scream.

Then I scream again.

I scream and scream and scream and can't stop screaming...

* * *

"Bandit! Wake up!"

My wife is shaking me.

"You're having a nightmare!"

I turn to her.

"I dreamed I was human. It was horrible." I'm hoarse from screaming.

"Look in my eyes," says Bandit. (Her name is also Bandit.)

I look at my reflection in her eyes. I see my cute black nose and whiskers and pointed ears and sharp teeth and darker fur around my eyes that gives me the name Bandit—gives every one of us the name Bandit, actually—and I am comforted.

I manage a small laugh. She strokes the fur on my ringed tail with her long nails.

"And," I continue, "in my dream squirrels and bears and flowers could talk."

"That's just silly," she says.

"Must've been something I ate. Human garbage that had gone bad."

"Hush now," says my beautiful raccoon wife, and we both return to dreamland.

IN THE RESTROOM OF MY MIND

The restroom attendant turned on the taps and adjusted the temperature. Hot, but not uncomfortably so.

"This is perfect. Thank you."

"You're welcome, sir. Soap?"

He squeezed a dab of liquid soap into the palm of my left hand. It smelled of lavender, not floral girly lavender but manly bracing lavender, making me feel like a warrior.

"Thank you."

"You're welcome, sir."

The pressure was on. I wanted to wash my hands faultlessly. I wanted to do it for him, this stranger who I felt I'd known all my life.

He handed me paper towels. He thought of everything.

"Thank you."

"You're welcome, sir." Did he approve? I think he did. It made me feel complete, in a way my father never did.

"What's your name?" I said.

"Reggie."

Right then and there I wanted to make up a song called "Reggie."

"Hello, Reggie. I'm Jim."

"I know."

Had I told him my name? I probably did and just forgot. Moving to the wood-paneled door, I hesitated. Something powerful drew me back into restroom, to the display of gum and combs and mints on the counter at Reggie's elbow. My eyes lingered for a split second on a bright yellow stick.

"Juicy Fruit. From Chicago," said Reggie.

"Ah. Chicago."

"Yes, Jim."

Muted sounds of the busy restaurant seeped in from outside the door. But Reggie and I were meeting on another plane. What should I say next? How did I begin to tell Reggie of my hopes and fears?

"Cologne, sir? To cover up the stench of your low self-esteem?"

"Well, maybe just a quick spray."

I examined the blue and green and gray bottles, my mind racing. Did he say what I thought he said?

I chose Paco Rabanne Invictus.

"Will this cover the stench of my low self-esteem?"

"I expect so, Jim."

I sprayed my wrists and both sides of my neck.

"Breath mint," said Reggie, "for the bullshit you spew out of your big fat mouth?"

"Pick one for me."

He gave me a green one. As I sucked on it I considered the BS I spew out of my big fat mouth, mostly at work. Reggie must've meant the things I say to make myself sound important. I'm a library technician—okay, a librarian, I spewed a little BS just then.

"Julie hates it when you talk that crap. I'm telling you for your own good, Jim."

I was interrupted by the arrival of another man, younger than me and in better shape. He peed courageously, resonantly. When he moved to the sink, I could see the lavender soap Reggie gave him was nicer than the soap he gave me, some secret lavender soap Reggie kept under the sink for guys who worked out. I could also see by the glance Reggie shot me he thought the young guy could give me some pointers on hand washing.

"I do fifty crunches before my coffee each morning," I said, after the young guy had tipped a dollar and split. "I may not have a beach body, but I can sit at a desk for eight hours without back pain."

"Be quiet and have another mint."

I sat on the edge of the sink and sucked on a white one.

"How do you know about Julie?"

"I know a few things."

"Like where they make Juicy Fruit?"

Reggie snapped a wet rag and hit me in the side of the face. *THWACK.* Ouch.

"Don't be sarcastic. Makes you look weak."

"Sorry."

Reggie realigned the combs on the counter.

"You two are on your third date. You like her, she likes you, but you're both wary. You think she might be too kooky."

"She tells me I look like a lemur with glasses, then giggles. And tonight . . ."

"Tonight you were shocked when she showed up with her friends, Heather and Craig. Talk about kooky, those two are off the charts," said Reggie, shaking his head. "Heather carries a purse that looks like a slice of pepperoni pizza, and so does Craig."

"It's brutal."

"I feel you, man. Heather makes her own jewelry out of plastic fruit. Craig wears cat's-eye glasses. They won't stop talking about Mexican wrestling movies. They say, 'Aces!' 'Keen!' 'Togged to the bricks!' 'Sweet patootie!'"

How did he know? He simply knew.

"Why are they here, Reggie?"

We were interrupted by a chunky fellow who entered and took ten minutes at the urinal, probably because Reggie and I were staring at him. He did a poor job washing his hands, just passing them under the water for a couple seconds, then drying them on his pants. He waddled to the door.

No. That's not how you behave in Reggie's world. I grabbed the portly intruder by his lapels.

"What's wrong with you? Pay the man."

"Sorry."

He fumbled for his wallet, dropped a dollar in Reggie's tray, then departed.

"I like the way you handled that, Jim."

My chest swelled. For Reggie, I would grab a thousand portly men.

He motioned me to come closer; he spoke quietly and confidentially.

"It's a good sign, Julie's friends being here. She's thinking about sleeping with you but wants reassurance from them that she's doing the right thing."

Of course. There was hope.

"But why do they have to be so obnoxious? Out of nowhere they'll start singing the theme from *The Love Boat*."

"Suck it up." He slapped me. "Stop cowering in the restroom and get back out there."

His words stung more than the slap. But he was right. There's a fine line between getting advice from a restroom attendant and cowering. I had crossed that line.

I took a twenty-dollar bill out of my wallet and placed it in Reggie's tray.

"Twenty dollars too much?" I said.

"No, that's good. Leave it—wait."

I paused on my way out. Reggie rose from his seat, straightening his tie and donning his jacket and porkpie hat.

"I'll put in a good word for you. Wait here."

"You just said I was spending too much time in the restroom."

"You are. And they'll want to know why. I'll tell them how you made the fat guy give me a dollar. I'll say, 'Is that the action of a man with low self-esteem?'"

"You'd do that for me?" Reggie nodded. I tipped him another twenty.

"I'll come with you," I said.

"No. That changes the dynamic. Stay here and do my job."

Wait. What? Suddenly I was driving in the fog without headlamps.

"But . . . multitasking . . . learning curve . . ."

Reggie slapped me again.

"Say 'learning curve' again and I'll use my fist."

And Reggie was gone.

I inspected the area around the sink. Reggie's workstation was like reading a sign in a foreign language, with mints and combs instead of words.

I realized someone might come in any second. I practiced worst-case scenarios on myself: scalding my hands with hot water, squirting soap on the floor, forgetting where Juicy Fruit came from.

I couldn't do this. I locked the door. Let them use the ladies' room, they'd be saving a life. *My* life.

My hand was on the latch when an officious businessman in a three-piece suit barged in. He squeezed past me, mumbling, "Excuse me," like I was an insect.

He did his thing at the urinal, whistling in an arrogant nonmusical way.

Then he crossed to the sink, looking around impatiently.

"Where's the guy?"

"I'm the guy."

"Then turn on the damn water."

How did I do it? How did I rise to the occasion? I thought of mothers lifting cars off their infants. Or was it infants lifting cars off their mothers? Regardless, I felt powerful, like an infant and a mother combined.

I turned on the water, making it hot but not uncomfortably so.

Three-Piece Suit got his hands wet.

"Soap?" I asked.

I squirted the ordinary lavender soap into his hands, not the really great lavender soap, which I didn't think he deserved because he was rude.

"Thanks," he managed.

"You're welcome, sir."

He washed his hands. He took his time and did a good job, and—did he really glance at me, looking for approval?

I gave him paper towels.

"Thank you," he said, this time with more conviction.

"You're welcome, sir. Chewing gum? Juicy Fruit is one of the best. It's from Chicago."

"Why the hell should I care?"

I'd gone too far. I'd gotten drunk with power.

Three-Piece Suit pulled a single out of his money clip and dropped it in the tray, then headed for door.

"Breath mint? For the BS you spew out of your big fat mouth?"

He froze. He did a slow-burning turn.

I grabbed a comb in case I had to defend myself.

"You're a cocky son of a bitch, aren't you?"

"Yes, sir."

"You're testing my limits. You're fearless."

"If you say so, sir."

"I like that in a restroom attendant."

Three-Piece Suit drew a twenty out of his money clip and dropped it in the tray.

"Thank you, sir."

He winked at me like we belonged to same club. Then he was gone.

For the next hour I was in the Zone. Men passed through my realm in slow motion. I knew instinctively the time each visitor would take to wash his hands and the color of mint he'd choose.

Guys were returning to the restroom three, four times, whether they had to pee or not, just to watch me work.

I wished my dad could have seen me. He'd say, "So you're a good restroom attendant, big deal," and I'd say, "Yes, Dad, it *is* a big deal," and then he'd turn to leave and I'd say, "Tip me, you wretched bastard who made me feel two inches tall all my life."

Frankly, it was a letdown when Reggie returned.

"Look at you," he said. "You look like you won the lottery."

I had been grinning so much my jaw muscles ached.

And Reggie had changed too. He wore cat's-eye glasses. He carried a Ninja Turtles lunchbox.

He put his hand on my shoulder. "Sorry, man. Bad news is, Julie isn't going to sleep with you."

I think he expected the news to bother me more than it did.

"Is there good news?"

Reggie nodded. "Me and Julie and Heather and Craig are going to the Museum of Candy Corn."

I didn't care. My future was here, with soap and colognes.

"Look after everything, Jim."

"You can trust me. I hope you and Julie get something going."

"I bet we do. Craig and Heather think I'm a sweet patootie."

He dropped a dollar in my tray, then bounced out of the restroom singing:

Love, exciting and new, come aboard, we're expecting you . . .

Reggie's exit created a breeze that scattered the mints. I rearranged them by color. I made it look easy.

GOD INVENTS THE LIGHTBULB

And lo, God didst look upon the earth he hath made, and the men and women he hath made also who dwelleth upon the earth, and God saw only corruption.

And the corruption God saw was not only political, which was to be expected, but also a more generalized corruption, leading to fornication and violence and other unseemly behaviors.

And rather than fix each instance of corruption singly, God chose to make it easier on himself by killing everyone at once.

And God saw that one man on earth was righteous, and his name was Noah. And Noah had three sons, who were called Shem, Ham, and Japheth.

And God appeared unto Noah and sayest, "You are righteous, and much adored by the angels in the Kingdom of Heaven."

And Noah sayest, "Lord, why dost thou butter me up?"

And God didst laugh a nervous laugh and sayest, "I'm going to destroy the earth." And God commanded Noah to make an ark of cypress wood, and the ark was to be three hundred cubits long and fifty cubits wide.

And after God reminded Noah to breathe, Noah sayest, "That's a lot of ark for me and my sons and our wives."

And God's nervous laugh didst go up an octave, and he sayest, "You shall share the ark with two of all living creatures, male and female."

And after twenty-four hours of unrighteous cursing, Noah grudgingly set about ark building and creature gathering.

And God prepared a flood to destroy the corrupt people of the world. And he thought it would be good if before the wicked people drowned, they had their skin burned off by hot rain passing through the hell of Gehenna. And God made sure Noah knew about the hot rain, so he'd be grateful and stop acting so pissy.

And God didst flood the earth for forty days. And Noah and his sons and their wives and two of every creature were safe in the ark, even though after day two they were driving each other up the wall with the sounds of their chewing.

And after forty days God caused the floodwaters to recede. And God sent unto Noah a dove, as a symbol of peace and a promise he would never again destroy the people of the earth. And Noah sayeth, "We already have two doves. Thanks for nothing."

And Shem, Ham, and Japheth didst lie with their wives and repopulate the earth.

But after two generations, the people were corrupt again, even worse than the first time, for they had selective amnesia about the hot rain.

And God wondered what had gone wrong, wondering if his destruction had been destructive enough.

And God decided to once again destroy the earth, and he sayest, "This is worse than being a homeowner and having to repaint every five years."

And though he hated to impose, God appeared once again unto Noah, who was much older but still righteous.

And as before, God commanded Noah to build an ark for himself and his great-great-grandsons who were called Todd, Brett, and Ryan. And God sayest unto Noah, "I shall once again destroy the earth, and forget I sent that dove because everybody makes mistakes."

And Noah didst build another ark, which was easier this time because he had kept the blueprints.

And God didst send upon the earth a torrential flood of whipping cream. And he didst enjoy seeing corrupt people dog paddle, thicken the cream, and go under.

But this time there was corruption aboard the ark. For Todd, Brett, and Ryan were not righteous, and they didst create a betting pool to see who could perform the most abominations with the creatures of the ark.

And after forty days, God caused the whipping cream that covered the earth to recede.

And he sent to Noah as a symbol of peace, not an attractive dove, for God had heard about Todd, Brett, and Ryan's betting pool, but instead a sooty pigeon.

And the earth was now populated with the offspring of Noah's great-great-grandsons and the animals of the ark, offspring that belonged in a sideshow.

And God was greatly frustrated, wondering how to get through to mankind.

And in an effort to distract himself, God didst make of the clay of the earth a cellular phone, which didst playeth a short melody.

And God answereth, saying, "How did you get this number?"

And a voice sayeth, "Lord, you were on my cold-call list. My name is Matt Zen-Albers, I'm a qualified life coach, and I'm here to help."

And God was taken in by Matt Zen-Albers's rapport-building skills. And God didst share his frustration of creating the earth and destroying it and destroying it again, and so forth.

And Matt Zen-Albers sayest, "You miss one hundred percent of the shots you don't take."

And God, failing to see how that applied, sayest, "I didst enjoy the whipping cream."

And Matt Zen-Albers sayest, "That's creative. Do more of that."

And so God didst repeatedly destroy the earth by flooding it with, in succession, vegetable broth, paint thinner, sweet tea, brake fluid, saliva, Gatorade, blood, urine, and cask ale.

And Noah sayeth, "To hell with it," and moved into the ark full-time.

And God sayest over coffee to Matt Zen-Albers, "I have repeatedly destroyed the earth, and yet when the earth is restored it is more corrupt than before."

And Matt Zen-Albers sayest, "The best way out is always through. Don't fear failure but rather fear not trying. . . ."

And the voice of Matt Zen-Albers began to sound unto God like the buzzing of a gnat.

And God didst realize that repeated destruction of the earth had not caused an end to corruption, plus he was running out of ideas for fluids.

And God didst think that he was too quick to reject fixing each instance of corruption individually, and that one-on-one is the best way after all.

And when Matt Zen-Albers didst present his bill to God for life-coaching services, God didst cause a localized cloud of whipping cream to appear and fall only on the place where sat the life coach.

And Matt Zen-Albers didst thrash about in the whipping cream, all the while saying, "I think I can, I think I can," until he drowned.

And God looked across the table at what he hath wrought, and saw that it was good.

ONE DAY SOON I'LL TAKE MY SHIRT OFF IN PUBLIC

My shirt is coming off. It's going to happen. The big day looms large. And then, there I'll be, naked to the waist, available for unrestricted viewing.

I am almost nearly fully mentally prepared for this event.

Why, you may ask, has it taken so long for me to feel secure enough to remove my top, thereby allowing strangers to scrutinize my man boobs?

Maybe you think I think I'm repugnant, or maybe I really am repugnant, or maybe a combination of both.

Guess what? I used to believe I was repugnant, but not anymore. Now I simply believe I'm unalluring, which is easier to live with.

So what's taken so long? What have I feared?

It's been a gradual process. Ironically, the more I resembled a bush gorilla, the greater my self-acceptance.

Now I realize I need not compare myself to others, except for that guy over there with the flabby belly hanging down over his belt buckle. I like him. I'll call him Arnie. I want him around for the big reveal.

Not that I'm obsessing about my moobs, but here's another thought: I'd like you to consider my ample tits a physical manifestation of the commonality I share with womankind. I, too, know the discomfort of attracting unwanted stares when running along the beach in slow motion. And though I may never suckle a babe, if I ever did I'd probably attract even more stares than women, especially if I attempt to suckle while running along the beach in slow motion. Please keep that in mind, womankind.

Also, look. Arnie's are bigger. Thanks, Arnie.

The location of the reveal is key. Where will it be?

The impact will be greatest if done in a busy public park, about 2 a.m., when the paths are filled with nocturnal joggers. I'll do it when the clouds part, under the blazing light of a waxing crescent moon.

Off comes the shirt, while I'm standing behind Arnie.

Then I'll step out.

The runners will halt and cheer. My bold gesture will inspire them, and they will follow suit. I will be hoisted onto the shirtless shoulders of an army of my grateful semiclothed brothers.

We'll march down the road, gathering followers in each small village. The highway will be littered with discarded Eddie Bauer piqué polos.

We'll arrive at the capital at daybreak, a hundred thousand strong. The transition of power will be peaceful. I will be anointed king. I won't wear a crown, because then people will stare at the crown and not at my garden-variety body. Arnie will be my jester, whispering in my ear, "All glory is fleeting, so gobble up that tub of caramel corn."

History will mark me a benevolent shirtless leader.

I will be asked to perform acts of gallantry, like feeding the poor or defending the kingdom against a bellicose enemy, and I will say, "Look at the unsightly anatomy I have exposed for you. Is that not enough?" and they will say, "Yes."

Mothers will celebrate their shirtless sons, and vice versa.

Wait. Maybe I'm rushing things. Maybe before I take my shirt off, I should work with a personal trainer. Just for a while, say six months, long enough to get a four-pack—I'm not greedy.

Say, I could be missing a bet by taking off my shirt before I'm really old. Can you imagine that? That would blow people's minds. People will say, "Look at that old fart with no shirt. He must have seen some stuff."

One day soon I'll take my shirt off in public. After the trainer. When I'm really old.

I hope you enjoyed *Giant Banana Over Texas*. Please consider leaving a review on Amazon, BookBaby Bookshop, Goodreads, or Barnes & Noble.

You can join my mailing list at <u>www.marknutter.com</u>.

I also wrote this book, available wherever collections of dark, absurd tales are sold:

"*Sunset Cruise on the River Styx* is a hilarious view into the void, where only the bravest, maddest comics go." Dennis Paoli, screenwriter. *Re-Animator, From Beyond.*

ABOUT THE AUTHOR

MARK NUTTER grew up in a motel near Joliet, Illinois, which is not as glamorous as it sounds. He's been published in *Havok*, *Mystery Weekly*, *Dear Leader Tales*, and the *Daily Drunk Magazine*. He's written a short fiction collection (*Sunset Cruise on the River Styx*). Mark has also written for the stage (*Re-Animator: The Musical*, *The Bicycle Men*, *Christmas Smackdown*), television (*Saturday Night Live*, *3rd Rock from the Sun*), and film (*Almost Heroes*). <u>www.marknutter.com</u>.